DEVIL SEEKER

CYCLE DEVILS MC WEST FLORIDA

by

Clare Power

Copyright

Devil Seeker, Cycle Devils MC #1

© 2015, Clare Power

ISBN-13:978-1508716600

ISBN-10:1508716609

Cover Designer: Margreet Asselbergs

Formatting by KBK Publishing

CYCLE DEVILS
FLORIDA

DEDICATION

Dedicated to the memory of

William E. Twardokus

July 25, 1940 – August 14, 2014

The real Backfire

I am sorry that he never got to see the finished book, but I am proud beyond words that he liked the blurb that was written and enjoyed the parts that were written before his sad passing.

I am honoured that he allowed his road name to be used for this book.

I pray that he Rides Free, Always.

SPELLING AND WORDS

Hi Folks

I have written this book mainly from two people's points of view – Kat and Backfire's. Kat is English and Backfire is American. This being the case you will notice some spelling differences I have deliberately put in to emphasise this...

Kat will spell words like this, colour and flavour, whilst Backfire will spell them like this, color and flavor.

Also, some words have different meanings in the two cultures:

1. Panties are knickers
2. Pants in English are generally old-fashioned full briefs, i.e. granny knickers/pants

3. Pants in America are trousers in England
4. Jeans are jeans wherever
5. Birmingham is the second largest city in England, commonly called Brum. Someone from that area is often known as a Brummie. They may well have a distinct local accent.

If I use slang terms, either English or American, I will try to explain them in the text of the book.

I hope this makes sense and adds to your enjoyment of the book.

Clare

KAT'S PROLOGUE

I guess you could say that I'm a bit of a dreamer. On a midweek evening, one of my favourite ways to relax is to read and get lost in different worlds, especially biker fiction. Most of these stories revolve around a woman who get kidnapped and end up being rescued by a sexy biker. These things may not be true, but it sure does make me wish they were. I mean, where is my knight in black leathers, riding up to rescue me on his Harley? I want a hero.

Most of the women in these books fall into a few basic types: the everyday, ordinary lady who falls for the MC biker, or the MC Princess looking for a bloke in a different club. Last, but not least, are the sweetbutts, or whatever term used to call a club whore who's looking for anyone who will have her.

Part of the reason I love to get lost in these books is because I will never be any of these women. I consider myself a biker in my own right, which means I don't imagine that in my real life I will ever get my very own fantasy lover, but I sure wouldn't mind finding a *real man*.

I'm what you would call fussy when it comes to men. It's just not my way to accept anything less than what I consider to be perfect. I'm now independent and financially secure. I have a sweet ride and I'm used to taking care of myself. I'm in my early thirties – thirty-two to be exact – but I think I look better now than I did when I was younger. It's amazing what confidence in yourself can do. My body may be shorter and curvier than the whole stick figure look that's so popular at the moment, but I'm fit and healthy because I play sports and work hard. I don't do the gym because really, a running machine just isn't for me. I'm totally comfortable in my own skin and I have found that a lot of men see this as a challenge to their precious manhood.

I would like to share my time with someone and I'm certainly up for sex. The crux of the matter is finding the right man for me.

I want an alpha male who is big, strong, and confident in himself so that he won't be intimidated by a woman who uses her own brain and has a bit of backbone about her.

If he's tall, dark and handsome, that really wouldn't be a disaster. I want him to be taller than me, even when I'm in the highest boots I can wear. As I'm only five feet five inches tall, it shouldn't be hard to find a man who can wrap me up in his arms and hold me under his chin, right? He would have to be a hard worker because I don't think I'd do well with a lazy ass man or someone who thinks they can scrounge off me without doing his part in a relationship. Showering after sweating and working all day is a must for me. I know damn well what I fancy and I expect nothing less.

I don't understand why it has been so hard to find one up to this point, but I'm hoping that by moving to America, all that will change for me. Perhaps I should make a list. I'm good at those.

I really want a true biker who has been in the lifestyle for years and understands what it means because let's face it, there's not exactly one around every corner, especially one who is single, interested, and meets all my criteria. I guess time will tell.

BACKFIRE'S PROLOGUE

I'm fucked in the head in a big way. Nothing in particular is wrong, I'm just fuckin' bored.

Everywhere I turn there's pussy, but it's gotten to the point where I find myself not even wanting to be bothered with it.

I don't want a fuckin' relationship. I just want to fuck a girl and get gone. I've figured out that whether they are from the clubhouse or just some random woman, they are all looking for something more from me, especially if I go back for seconds. The ones in the club just want a man to latch onto and be his old lady while ones outside the club have this fucked up illusion of what it means to be with a biker because of some fucking TV show. Bitches are straight up losing their minds trying to romanticise this lifestyle.

I work my ass off every day and I have the body to prove it. I don't shave or cut my hair until I get annoyed with it. I wear clothes that are comfortable and practical – not based on fashion – and I *always* wear my colors when I'm out on my bike.

I'm a member of the Cycle Devils MC—West Florida, and I expect to be treated as such.

We are 1%ers. That doesn't mean that we are involved in organized crime, but it separates us from the other boring 99% of motorcyclists. In my world, they don't get the title of biker. You have to earn that right from us.

A lot of us make most of our money through fairly legal means. I design custom bikes that most people find fuckin' unbelievable. I certainly charge enough for them and I pay my dues to the club, just like the rest of the brothers. That's not saying I've never done anything illegal for the club, just that I can prove to the cops that I have a legitimate source of income.

My life is great, but it would be fuckin' perfect if I could find a woman who's just down to fuck. Why is that so much to ask?

CHAPTER 1
FRIDAY NIGHT AT THE ALLIGATOR

Kat

I walk into the local biker bar feeling good. Tonight the plan is to have a bit of fun with my new friend Amber and check out part of the local scene.

Unlike the bars people imagine all bikers frequent, the Alligator is not a dirty, dingy dump. You can walk in as a girl on your own without having to have sex in the back room. It's clean and modern with a large range of different beers and great food. Rock music plays low enough to talk to someone close, but loud enough to enjoy. Not a bad place for a night out.

Sitting at the bar, I survey the crowd and find that the place is buzzing. It says something when no matter how packed the place is, you can still manage to snag a seat, but what it says is another matter.

I look the part tonight. I stuffed my leathers and helmet in the saddlebags, leaving me in my Harley tank that shows off a little cleavage, denim shorts and cowboy boots. The Florida weather still feels too hot to me after sunny old England.

I remove the plait from my hair that I put in to avoid helmet hair; keeping the tangles down and the bugs out. My hair is long and red, with even a bit of a kink from the plait. My eyes are a sort of mix of green and brown, but they suit me. I'm not a great one for makeup, but I keep my eyebrows waxed and tinted dark, along with my eyelashes tinted black for a bit of pop. A lot of makeup doesn't work with the wind in your face on a bike. I'm more than happy with the way that I look and I'm not afraid to show it.

Amber comes up and snags the empty bar stool next to me and we order Diet Cokes. I met Amber in the local craft shop. After the first few times of bumping into each other in the yarn aisle, we started to chat as people with obvious common interests do, and that was that. We've even begun setting a night aside once a week where we do nothing but craft. She is American and has lived in Florida for years, so she is the perfect guide for me on how to live in the States.

"Hey lady. How are things?" I ask.

"Pretty good. Work was good today and I'm planning to get my house updated. You're becoming a bad influence on me," Amber looks around and laughs, "This place is five minutes from my house and I've never been here before."

I grin at her, "It's not really your type of place. Thanks for coming and keeping me company."

To say Amber's not a biker in any way, shape, or form is no exaggeration, but she likes me for me so that's all I need. Like me, she is in her thirties, but she's slim with medium brown hair that has dramatic natural silver streaks running through it and green eyes. I'm on a a manhunt and Amber is offering me moral support, and for that, I'm grateful. Although this is obviously a biker bar, it isn't the sort of place where people look funny at her even though she's obviously a non-biker.

We look around at the Alligator's clientele, which is a varied mix of people. Many are clinging to the title of biker by a very thin thread. Not all bikers are made from the same cloth.

"There sure is quite a mixture of folks here tonight. What do you think? Could any of the men here be what you're looking for?" she asks.

A quick look around doesn't give me any hope.

"Don't look so sour, Kat. I'm your wing woman for the night so if you tell me what sort of biker you're into, I can help you keep a lookout."

Now that is a good question, so for the next few hours over dinner we discuss the type of men considered to be bikers. Does the title biker only apply to the outlaw? The member of a proper 1% motorcycle club who is so immersed in that culture that he lives, works, and breathes only the club lifestyle. What of the club member who works a nine to five job? There is also the lone wolf who rides and has no association to a club, but lives to ride nonetheless. Is he not considered a biker just because he has no affiliations with a club?

We continue to go on with no real answer, but regardless of all the different types of people who ride, in all the different types of lifestyles, it's still all centred around one item; the motorcycle. The biker scene is quite diverse, so I suppose anyone who wants to call himself, or herself, a biker, is to some degree a biker. The problem that I'm having is what type of biker would really interest me?

"I have no real idea. Before this conversation, I thought I had some idea of what I was looking for, but breaking it down like this, I see that I really don't know now. All I do know is that I want a hardworking man who wants me for all of me, and I think I'll know him when I see him. I won't settle for anything less than what I feel I deserve, and that's something that won't change, no matter what type of biker he turns out to be. Just no mopeds," I finish with a giggle.

I have a look around at the single men and see that putting pressure on a situation will only end in failure. It was an unrealistic fantasy of mine, believing that leaving England and coming to America I would find the perfect biker for me; like he would just fall into my lap and that would be that. I have set my bar too high with getting what I want right now so I have to take a step back and just let it happen. I've heard the saying that if you're looking for something, you won't find it. It's only when you least expect it that it finds you. The only thing to choose from here tonight are tourists who will be heading out soon, back to their lives somewhere else.

So Friday night at the bar is a bust on the man front, but I've enjoyed hanging out with Amber and that's good enough for me.

Backfire

I pull up to The 'Gator with some of my brothers. We sit in the parking lot, checking out the scene. The fuckin' place seems full of tourists, not women looking for a good time. Well shit. No point in even getting off our bikes. Better luck at the clubhouse, I guess.

CHAPTER 2
FIRST ENCOUNTER AT THE DIY STORE

Kat

I have to admit that I am very lucky. I've just moved to Florida, to a little town north of St. Petersburg. The best bit is that because my Parentals are downsizing, they sold the big old family house to buy a much smaller bungalow, and in the process, handed over some of those pennies to my sister Jack and me. Thanks to their generosity and my savings, I bought a house of my very own, making me rent and loan free. I even have money in the bank to start my own business when I'm ready.

My new house has a master bedroom, or maybe that should be a mistress's bedroom, with a huge shower big enough for two in the en-suite. There is a lounge diner with a fabulous integral kitchen and doors off to the small garden and the garage. Down a corridor from the lounge is what some might call the guest wing of the house, but I have made that part of my home into a craft room and library. It also has a bathroom with a corner spa bath. These may not have been the room designations the estate agents sold the house as, but I made them to work for me. After all, it's mine – all mine.

Some people might think of Florida in terms of hell with the heat, humidity, and hurricanes, but not me. After living in England for the past twenty years or so, with its entertainingly unpredictable weather, I'm ready for all the sun I can get.

I'm in the process of gradually redecorating my new home also. I love red walls and I want at least one bright wall in every room, so that's how I find myself in the paint aisle at the DIY store, but the paint isn't the only thing that has my interest.

At about six feet four inches tall with dark curly hair, neat beard and moustache, this man is not Hollywood model handsome, but he is handsome in a rough sort of way. His body is tan from the sun and he is built like a man who works hard with well-defined, lean muscles. Yum.

He is dressed in biker boots, blue jeans and a black sleeveless t-shirt that says, *Support Your Local Cycle Devils.* His right arm has an amazing sleeve of tribal tattoos while his left arm is covered in coloured tattoos. If ever a man looked like a biker God, it would absolutely be him.

See? I wasn't even looking and he found me.

I don't know much about the local motorcycle club or MC, the Cycle Devils, but I do know that it shouldn't be hard to find general information about them on the internet. I would really like to know how well they work together and how they treat their women. I know that this type of information will be harder to come by. The bottom line is that if I meet them, I want to learn about them slowly, not jump in with both feet and repent at leisure.

What I *do* know of MC's is that they live in a tightly controlled world of their own. They have very clear ideas of respect and enforce things within their world, and the women who live with these men are also ruled by their ways. The women don't know an awful lot – if anything – about the club's business and have no vote in what the club does. There are only two choices for women; either live with it or move along. Most women love the lifestyle and have as much loyalty to the club as their men do.

I will admit that the downside to that is that the women associated with most clubs seem to follow a set rule of no mixing outside the club. They don't talk to men outside the club, even old friends.

I've seen the ladies of men in one MC sit in a corner of a pub, talking amongst themselves while their men were elsewhere in the bar, not drawing attention to themselves. No dancing, no pool, not even talking to their men and having their drinks delivered by a prospect. All I could think was how sad and boring their lives must be. This is one of the reasons that I don't want a biker that belongs to an MC. That's not a lifestyle that I want for myself.

Until I know more about the Cycle Devils, I'm going to be a bit careful. Anyhow, just because he's wearing a support tee doesn't mean he's actually a member of the MC. I mean, he's not wearing a leather cut, patches, or colours.

I'm so lost in thought that I forget that I'm blatantly staring at him when he turns and looks me over. Please let him like what he sees because make no mistake, he's one fine looking man. Please do not let me be drooling.

To speak or not to speak, that is the question, but the faint of heart never won a sexy man such as him.

"Hello. I'm sorry, I didn't mean to stare. I was looking at your shirt," I say, full of originality.

He looks at me for another minute and gives me a chin lift, beckoning me closer to him. I normally don't like this type of arrogance from a man. It would send me running in the other direction or getting in his face about it, but my body is doing the thinking for me as I make my way toward him.

"You saying you like bikers, babe?" It's a fair question. After all, so many non-biker types wear biker clothing as a fashion statement, especially the Harley brand so I nod in response.

"Words, babe. Always give me words," he orders softly.

"Yes," I respond, breathless.

"The Cycle Devils are organizing a charity run and party at the clubhouse next Saturday. Wanna come?".

I'd heard about the run next weekend and actually picked up a flyer for it earlier. The run is to raise money to help a local lad with mobility issues and his family by trying to supply him with a new wheelchair. It's also to help with conversion issues in the family home. I'd been planning to go anyway, but now I had another excuse.

We haven't even exchanged names so I decide to fix that, "My name is Kat, Katrina," I offer.

"Backfire."

I smile at that, finding the options as to why he has this for a road name amusing. I raise a questioning eyebrow just as he raises his own, but he has a smug looking grin on his face. Looks like that is a discussion for later, if I decide that there is a later.

"Well it's nice to meet you, Backfire. Now, since we have that out of the way, how do you suggest we do this?"

"You can ride bitch with me." Something about his tone makes him sound like he's bestowing a great honour upon me.

"Or I could ride my own bike," I say with a cheeky grin. I know that a lot of people have their own ideas on who should go on the back of their bikes and I don't like being a pillion until I know a bloke's rules.

His eyebrows shoot up at this information, but then a slow, half-smile appears. "Or you could ride your bike. You could meet me at the clubhouse and we can ride out together, if that suits you."

I give him a nod. That will suit me just fine.

Backfire

I get to the store to pick up some paint because we're trying to fix the clubhouse up for the weekend. Really this is a job for a damn prospect, not me, but they are busy doing things I really don't fuckin' wanna do, so I decided this would be the easiest of the work to do.

The club has decided to make a real effort for the charity run next weekend, which includes dishing out all the jobs in the public areas of the clubhouse, inside and out. We're having new carpet installed and other crap like that. We're even fuckin' installing new toilet seats for the ladies. The outside is getting new paint, the yard is getting tidied up with the lawn being mowed. I don't understand why all this shit is being done, but there are even flowers being planted. What the fuck is that all about.

I'm not flying my colors in the store because I haven't come on my bike. The newer guys wear theirs when they're using cages, but I'm more old school than that.

This hot ass bitch next to me in the aisle has me thinking. I can see her staring at me from the corner of my eye and what can I say, I have a dick and I wanna give her a ride. Problem is I'm busy at the clubhouse, helping get everything ready for the rest of the week.

I beckon her over anyway and she obeys me instantly. That shit always works. Can't be fuckin' with bitches who wanna play games. I just wanna have some fun and move on. It's not fuckin' hard.

I'll have her for the weekend. She can be my reward to myself for all the hard work I put in this week. I'd even put her on my bitch seat, and I'm fuckin' fussy about who goes there. The bitch has to be hot to be seen with me.

I kindly invite her to join me when she tells me she has her own bike. Then she fuckin' challenges me again by telling me her name before I bother asking for it. Fine. I can deal with that shit because my cock wants some of her. After I fuck her she'll be gone 'cause not only does a bitch have to be hot to be seen with me, but she has to be somethin' special for me to fuck her a second time. I don't do complicated.

I tell her to meet me at the clubhouse and hope to fuck she doesn't turn up on a fuckin' rice burner 'cause if she does, then I'll have to educate her on what a real bike is.

My cock is getting hard just looking at her and that accent is hot as hell. I think I might want her for

more than one go, but we'll see how she does the first time around. All I have to do is train her on the right way to behave around me.

We both go our separate ways to get what we came for and I want to kick my own ass for not asking her to meet me sooner. A week seems like a long fuckin' time to wait, but the moment has passed as I watch her leave the store. I'm sure I can find something to take the edge off until the weekend. The new blonde that's been hanging around the clubhouse will have to do.

CHAPTER 3
A BIT ABOUT ME

Kat

With my Dad being American and my Mom being English, that gives me dual nationality, but even though I'm technically as American as I am English, it feels like I have a new country because I've lived in England for so long. I think I'm settling in quite nicely, especially with the excitement of being here, owning a house here, and exploring it all on my Softail Slim. It's the sexiest bike in the world with really low, uncluttered lines. I can touch the ground with both feet when I'm sitting on it and let me tell you, that is a very rare thing at my height. I usually find that even if a bike has a low seat, most of them are so wide that it makes it hard to touch the ground. I'm taking my time and

riding for a few hours at a time when I get the chance; learning the area and finding different routes home.

I pull on my leather trousers because who wants road rash if there were an accident? My jacket and helmet are next and I'm on my bike, ready to go.

As I ride, I start to think about how my life has been up 'til now, making me into the woman I am. The bare bones of growing up saw me as a happy child; a bit quiet though, and never truly fitting in with the other kids. My sister, Jacqueline, or Jack as she's known, was an exception. She understood me and what I liked, and apparently, we liked the same things. We had plenty of variety growing up in two countries that were similar, yet hugely different in culture and language. It was like always having the best, and worst, of both worlds.

I thought as a child that I had it hard, but when I look at it now, I realize how incredibly lucky I've been. So many people have wretched, twisted childhoods, but not me. In fact, I have to admit that I was spoilt rotten.

Even as I got older, I never mixed with the cool crowd or got into fashion. I never went to the popular parties, or any parties for that matter, and I never listened to the same music that everyone considered popular. I was the outsider; the strange girl who liked rock music, didn't follow the trends and went her own way. I studied art at Uni which I found was way easier than school. Being able to pick your own courses and mix with more people who had a similar sort of interest as you was at least a step in the right direction.

Then came my first baby steps into my true life. After Uni I moved to Birmingham, technically to find work, but I found more than that. Outside of the semi-protected college digs, I ended up sharing a house with two other girls, both into the biker scene and they showed me what I wanted in my life. The first time I walked into the local biker bar I was in lust with the music, the people, and most importantly, the roar of the bikes. My life became a pattern of working during the week and partying the weekends away. Best times of my life.

I learnt that I wanted to use my artistic talent to paint bike tanks. It started by me looking at bikes on runs and at rallies when I was a pillion on my ex-boyfriend's bike. It all came into sharp focus for me when I saw an exhibition of bike tanks in a museum. The sheer beauty and diversity really spoke to me.

I passed my bike test on a 125cc, as you do now in the UK, and moved swiftly on upwards to a BSA A10. It was considerably lighter than some of the Japanese bikes available and it didn't need too much work to be able to touch the floor. I loved the look of it and never did play with the paintwork on it. I just figured it had been around longer than me so that had to be worth something, or at least it was to me.

I buried myself in all things biker then spent the next few years realising what parts of the lifestyle actually suited me best. To be a biker is to be free, and I felt free to choose my own path, but all that was years ago. Now it's time to think of the possibilities that are right here, right now for me.

Backfire

For some reason I find myself sitting alone outside the clubhouse at a picnic table, drinking a beer and wondering if it's time for me to get my own place instead of living here. It's not like I don't have the fuckin' money, but I don't know where the thought is coming from, either.

I suppose I stay because I'm used to the company. Dad's a biker and Mom goes with him for rides now, but that wasn't always the case. She had us, me and my two brothers to take care of and she made sure we had a stable home life where she was around all the time. Mom's the traditional type, as in she did the cooking, the cleaning, and looking after her boys. The house was Moms, which always stayed so clean and tidy, while the outbuildings were the men's territory where Dad had things set up for bike building and repair. My brothers and I learned to ride, probably before we could walk. We rode dirt bikes together all the time, anywhere we could, just as long we didn't go near Moms garden, hens or horses. I miss riding the horses because to me, it felt like a different type of freedom.

My dad was a Nomad for the Cycle Devils for years, but now he's settled into a home chapter in Louisville, where my brothers and I grew up. My brothers, Ultan and Seamus, are both fully patched members of the New Orleans chapter of the club. I live the life I was born to live and I love it. It would all be perfect if I could work out this feeling of being unsettled that's started to come over me lately.

Why am I bothering about where to live? If I see somewhere I like, I'll buy it. That fuckin' simple. Now as for who I fuck, I'm so fuckin' bored of all these whores hanging around here, so I'm happy as shit that I got that little redhead coming this week. I sure as fuck hope the bitch works out. Fucking should never have to be this hard.

CHAPTER 4

WEDNESDAY NIGHT

CRAFT SESSION... OR NOT

Kat

"It's really weird, Amber," I complain. "I've never had trouble from the Police, and now I'm getting visits from them every day. This is ridiculous!"

To say craft night is a bust tonight is an understatement. As soon as Amber got here, I opened the cider and got the chocolate out of the fridge. Calories don't count when you have company.

"So what exactly has been happening?" she asks as she settles down on the settee with her chocolate.

"It started on Sunday. I was painting my garage door when the Police came around. Apparently, they received a complaint about the noise of my bike. I explained to them that there is nothing I can do about it, as it's a standard Harley exhaust system. I mean, what's the problem? There are shedloads of Harleys around here. Surely they don't visit everyone who owns and rides a motorcycle."

"On Monday I went to this amazing second hand book store. I made some purchases and came home. I wasn't even home more than thirty minutes before the Police come around again with another noise complaint, only this time it's that I'm playing my music too loud, which I was not. I don't get it."

"Have you upset anyone recently?" Amber asks. "The Police have to come out every time there is a complaint and some people use them as a weapon, you know, as a means of harassing people they don't like."

Interesting point.

"The only thing that I've done is put in an application for a unit just up the road that I think will work as my new paint shop. Realistically how many people could know about that?"

"I don't know, but it might be useful to see if we can find out."

Amber leaves me with lots to think about over the next few days.

The pattern continues over Thursday and Friday, with the Police coming again for noise complaints.

I'm starting to get wound up by all the Police activity. I'm now researching correct local Police procedures and by-laws to make sure everything I am doing at home is correct, as well as how I am setting up my business. I suppose it all amounts to the same thing. I'm worried that the whole game of *"Let's keep reporting Kat to the Police"* will expand to the plans of opening my own shop.

All this really sucks, especially since I could be spending my precious time mooning over Backfire. I have to figure this out, and soon.

CHAPTER 5
CYCLE DEVILS MC
CHARITY RUN

Kat

Saturday arrives and I am really looking forward to seeing Backfire again. I've been enjoying a few fantasies where he has had the starring role, but they're only when I manage to sleep without worrying.

I've dressed biker hot, not biker slutty. I'm wearing my black leather chaps over a pair of jean shorts and a jacket over a Harley tank top. The jacket and helmet I wear are ones that I've painted myself, strangely enough with a snow leopard. It's a design that I've created to stand out from the black of my jacket. If my bike wasn't blue, I might have painted it to match as it would really work well with the lines of the bike. I complete my look with more make up than usual, but my glasses will stop the wind from getting in my eyes and I've plaited my damp hair in a couple of braids which will give it a little bit of body instead of parading around with flat helmet hair. I hope that Backfire is worth the effort I've invested in my look to impress.

I'll admit that I am a bit worried about his attitude. He seems a tad arrogant, but then again, he's a biker. What's the worst that can happen? I have my bike so if something goes down that I don't like, I can just leave if I want to.

Backfire

I roll out of bed on Saturday morning and hunt for some clean clothes. It's fuckin' early for me on a Saturday, but I'm looking forward to seeing that hot little redhead again. She better be worth it. I've been thinking about her all week and since I want her on my dick, I've decided to look past that little bit of attitude I saw in her. I'm thinking I might like her giving me that attitude while I let her ride me. It's gonna be a fuckin' good day.

Kat

The ride to the Cycle Devils clubhouse is pleasant enough. There is a big turnout of bikes with prospects there to allocate parking. It's all very organised and I like that.

When I approach, I'm pulled over by a prospect who obviously wants to flirt with me. I let him chat me up for a bit and when he asks if I'm here with anyone, I tell him that I'm meeting a man who called himself Backfire. That name causes his whole attitude to change and now he can't get away from me fast enough. He ends our conversation rather abruptly and points for me to park right up next to the clubhouse. Warning bells start to go off, but I'm too excited about riding today to think any more on it.

Oh shit.

This cannot be happening. There he stands in all his glory, wearing his cut with all his patches and his colours as he looks straight at me.

SHIT!

He wasn't wearing patches or colours the day I met him but here he is, an MC club member. I'm seriously considering turning around to leave and cut my losses. He is not the kind of biker I wanted to get mixed up with but as soon as we make eye contact, he beckons me over and I again find my body going straight to him. How in the hell does he do this to me?

As I make my way toward him, I make the decision to go through with the ride and leave as soon as it's over. As I get closer, I see every patch in detail. Not only is he a member of the Cycle Devils, he is a fully patched member too. My heart drops to my stomach in disappointment. Oh well, nothing I can do about it now except to suck it up and get it over with.

Backfire

I'm waitin' outside for this bitch and I'm pissed because this isn't how I usually play shit. My brothers would ride my ass if they realized what I was doing, but once I finally see her, I'm shocked as shit and my cock is instantly hard.

She's riding a Harley, which I'm thankful as fuck for. I've had a week to get my head around her riding her own bike and damn, if she doesn't look hot as hell riding it. She's wearing one of those big helmets with a cool ass drawing on it. I think she's gonna be a lot more than I bargained for. I'm fuckin' regretting that I let her walk out of the store last week without finding out a little more about her.

Not only is this bitch hot, but she's getting more interesting by the fuckin' second.

When she finally looks at me, she appears stunned. She looks like she's reconsidering, maybe even about to run but that's not fuckin' happening. I gesture with my hand for her to come to me and with that, I see her eyes flash and a new determination starts to take hold. I can tell she's strong minded already, but is she fuckin' prejudiced, too?

She approaches us, then hesitantly stops and hovers a few feet away from me so I open my arm to her and she comes to me. I can sense her reluctance, but she does it in spite of herself; a small victory in what might be an interesting war between us. I hug her close as soon as she's in my arms because I want to feel her close and help feel a little more comfortable. I wouldn't normally give bitches any clue that I might like them, but I want her to know that I'm interested.

My brothers look on, smirking. No fuckin' doubt they're storing this scene up for later fun at my fuckin' expense. Their eyes check her out and I know they see what I see. She's hot and they're diggin' her, but they don't comment. They wait to see where I am on this, showing me respect. I expect it, but appreciate it also.

"This is Kat, everyone." I say, kindly introducing her, "Kat, these are my brothers; CC, Shades, and Brewer."

She gives them a small smile, "Hello. It's nice to meet you all," she says. I see the boys get the idea behind why I like her.

"Hey, Babe." CC replies, "That's a hot fuckin' jacket."

Kat's smile turns to a full watt grin, "Cheers! I did the artwork myself."

"Where you from, girl? Hell of an accent you got there." Brewer asks.

"My dad is American while my mom is English. I've spent the last twenty odd years in England," she grins, "Just moved here about two months ago and I'm working to get myself sorted out."

I fuckin' love this, getting loads of info on her without it looking like I want to know. Glad my brothers are such nosey fucks.

"When you say you did the artwork, what did you mean?" asks Shades.

"I mean I design and paint things; custom tanks, helmets, leathers, even the occasional van. Just about anything like that, really. It's what I used to do in England and after I get situated here, I intend to open up a speciality paint shop. I do anything from pinstripes and flames to realistic stuff like these," she indicates the jacket and helmet, "to working on new techniques in 3-D art."

Well now she has everyone's attention. I don't know if I like that shit. Chances are that if the jacket and helmet are any sign of what she can really do, then she is fuckin' good and all my brothers will be interested in her. Fuck.

"Do you know what I do for a living?" I cut in.

"No."

"I design custom bikes, I have a degree in engineering design."

She gives me a broad smile and I know she's gonna be worth fucking more than once. I'm already way too interested in her for it to be a one-time deal anyway so I'm not exactly irritated at the idea of having her around for a while. In fact, the whole idea of Kat is beginning to sound better and better.

Kat

I swallow my disappointment at Backfire being in an MC and I'm strangely nervous as I approach him and his friends. They aren't really different, and yet they are. All MC's vary to some degree from each other and I don't know enough about the Cycle Devils to know exactly what to expect.

I stand slightly back from them, vaguely wondering what to do next when Backfire opens his arms to me. I walk into them, not wanting to make him look bad in front of his brothers, but I sort of like the idea of being in his arms too.

He holds me close to him as he introduces me to his friends and we begin a very normal conversation. I even start to relax in Backfire's arms and begin to look forward to the ride coming up. Maybe this is a good sign that they aren't as I had previously thought, but it would be irresponsible of me to let my guard down too soon.

The group begins to go off in separate directions, leaving me alone with Backfire. I stay in his arms without comment for another minute, just breathing in the scent of him. He smells of clean man; mint and leather. It's intoxicating.

"Hi," he smiles, turning me to face him in his arms.

"Hey yourself" I smile back. We're not exactly touching anymore now, but it wouldn't take much for us to be pressed together. After everything I've assumed about MC bikers, I can't believe I feel so turned on by this man. I can't let anything happen without knowing more, so I go for easy, "So how does this work?"

"The registration desk is over there, I'll come with you."

Backfire

I walk her over to the desk that's being manned by my brothers, Sock and OB. They are the two prospects that are closest to being patched in and they are our runners today.

"This is Kat and she's with me," I say to OB as he hands her a form and I hand over the money for her entry fee.

She looks at me in surprise but I raise my eyebrow and she backs down a bit. I hope it's because she has the brains to know to talk to me in private and not in front of my brothers. Yeah, I see it in her eyes that she didn't like the gesture, but tough. I'm impressed that she knows when to keep her mouth shut.

After she fills in the form and hands it over with a shy smile, she turns to walk back but I grab her arm and again, she doesn't say a word. She just waits for me to take care of my business and that to me is a fuckin' good sign.

Kat

What am I doing?

I'm just going to go with the flow. I won't say what's on my mind right now to him because I have enough sense than to cause him to think he is losing face in front of his brothers. One day, just get through this one day and it'll all be over.

Backfire pulls my arm for me to stop, turning me to face him as he states the obvious, "You did good in front of the guys by keeping your mouth shut about the money. Before you say anything, I asked you here today so I pay your entry fee. Three times now you've kept your thoughts to yourself and I can tell you hate not telling me where to shove it, but the fact that you aren't tells me a lot about you. You're doing good, babe."

With that, he lets my arm go and continues to lead me back to the group, "Since this is a charity ride, we aren't doing this in club order so you can ride next to me. I just need to know if you're used to riding in a group."

"Yes, I am. In England I used to go on a lot of charity rides, MAG runs, that sort of thing. I should have no bother being safe in a group."

"MAG?"

"Motorcycle Action Group, the British Riders' Rights Association. It mostly started out as a protest against helmet laws and now campaigns about laws that the powers that be in Europe want to bring in. I can be safe," I assure him.

"Alright then. You can ride with our group."

"It'll be an odd sort of date if we rode apart, don't you think?"

He stops and pulls me to face him, "I never thought of that. I don't date, and yet here we are."

"Well when someone asks you to meet them somewhere to do something with them, don't you consider that as asking someone out on a date? In my experience, that's how it's done, but I suppose it's of no matter. One date won't kill either one of us," I smile as we reach his bike.

It's a one of a kind custom-built bike that only has a solo seat, so I look at him and he grins, "I would have put a bitch pad on for you."

"Well I'm glad you didn't have to. It would have spoilt her lines."

He smirks, "Bring your bike over here, babe," so I nod and take off to fetch her.

I see others getting ready for the ride, so I do the same. I idle on my bike, ready to go as Backfire and his brother Shades make their way to me, letting most of their brothers go before tagging in at the back of their club in front of the prospects. At least there is another girl on a bike riding with the club, and others have girls on the back of their bikes so I'm feeling excited and confident right about now.

Backfire

Interesting. I've never considered asking a bitch to do something with me that didn't involve sex as a date but I sure as shit will accept that term with Kat. But if she thinks for one fuckin' second that she can just cut and run after the ride, she'll fuckin' learn that she's with me until I say she can go.

The ride goes great, but I'm only interested in the woman riding at my side. She does real good. She keeps up and I don't have to resort to pulling her out of the group onto a side street, using the prospect as a buffer between us and the main group.

I've got to know more about this woman. The more I watch her, the more I fuckin' want her.

Kat

I have no idea why I did it, but instead of doing the sensible thing at the end of the run like going home, I go back to the clubhouse with Backfire.

What on earth was I thinking?

We ride into the compound around the clubhouse, which literally is a big, old house. It stands in a very large plot with a privacy wall all the way around it. As well as the house itself, there are a couple of buildings clearly visible at the side. The front of the area is basically a huge parking area for all the bikes, with a few trucks spread throughout. Down the other side of the house is a grassy area leading out to what looks like a huge back garden.

I park my bike by the other woman who rode her own bike. She is a tall, blonde lady; beautiful and seemingly unselfconscious about it, making her all the more striking because of it. She rides a Harley Street Glide and I'm a bit envious. It's a beautiful bike.

"I'm Lori," she introduces herself, "the rest of the party is at the back of the clubhouse."

Lori doesn't need to tell me that she is with Brewer because she has patches on her back to say so. The top rocker says Cycle Devils, with the bottom patch saying Property of Brewer. Whatever works for her, I suppose.

"I'm Kat," I reply, "I was invited by Backfire."

She does a double take, but after a second passes, she nods and asks, "Do you want to go to the party straight away, or make a side trip to the ladies?"

"Ladies, please."

The clubhouse is not exactly what I imagined on the inside. It's fresh, clean, and bright, with what looks like fresh paint too. I quickly realise that this was probably the reason for Backfire's shopping trip at the DIY store the day I met him. The ladies room is also sparkling. It even has a loo roll and smells of bleach, which tells me they went to a lot of trouble to make this place clean and presentable.

Lori is quiet as we use the facilities and once we are finished, she leads me out the back where we walk toward the men who are waiting for us.

"What do you want to drink?" Backfire asks.

"Diet Coke, please."

He gets me my drink and grabs my hand to pull me along with him, taking me further around to the side of the clubhouse, past a no entry sign enforced by a prospect where I find that we are alone.

"Ok," he says, "let's be straight with each other. There was a problem when you saw me today, wasn't there? What the fuck was that all about?"

I decide honesty is the best policy. "I didn't realise you were in a motorcycle club, and to be honest, I was hoping you were just a regular biker, so I found myself a bit disappointed."

His eyes narrow on me. "Are you saying that you don't like my club?"

I get the idea that I need to tread carefully here. "It's not exactly your club that's the problem. I don't know your club or how it runs. I've met some members of motorcycle clubs before and it isn't a lifestyle that I would choose to live for myself is all."

Now he's visibly not pleased. "Have you ever hung out with a club?"

"No, just someone on the outside looking in."

"Did you like what you saw?"

"For the blokes, it looks like a great time, but for the women? Not so much. It all seemed so restrictive to me and that is not at all how I want to live my life," I say, but I don't meet his eyes. I'm stronger than this, or so I thought.

"So you are judging my club and me based on other clubs," he almost snarls.

"No, I'm not. Otherwise, I would have found some excuse to have left already– probably at the end of the ride." I quickly spit out. Now I'm able to look him straight in the eyes. I can see that he's a man who expects nothing less.

He nods, taking the conversation in and thinking it through.

"What are you going to do now?" He's not backing down for a second.

I look at him in surprise. "What do you mean?"

"I mean, I want you to stay with me tonight. In my bed," he smirks.

"Excuse me, but I hope I didn't hear you right," I say, shocked.

"Start thinking about it now and be ready to accept it. You're here with me and I expect to have you sooner rather than later." He waits for a moment and when I find I'm at a loss for words at his statement, he goes on, "Listen, we're both adults here and before you found out I was part of an MC, you agreed to meet me so you must have liked something about *me*, not my patch. I'm the same man you met a week ago." He's cocksure of himself and I like it, but there is no way in hell I'm going to inflate his ego any more than it already is.

"Look, Backfire. I admit that there is something about you; your good looks and the idea of you being a biker was what caught my interest. Today was a shock when I saw that you are not just a biker, but you belong to an MC, something that I have made a point of staying away from, but nevertheless, here I am, but my intentions obviously differ from yours. I was expecting to learn a bit about you and your club. I know how you men like to bed your women quickly and get them on their way in the same manner, so in answer to your question, I do like you, but I don't even know you. I didn't come here to have you tell me that I'm staying here to sleep with you. If I thought that was your intent, I never would have shown up today. I'm not going to be one of those women who just jump into bed with you because you say so. You have obviously picked the wrong woman and I'm sorry that you've wasted your time."

I get up to go when he grabs my arm, stopping me, "Stay with me tonight, Kat. We don't have to fuck, but I have every intention of getting to know you, and for you to get to know me."

Oh My God. Now What do I do?

"Well aren't you blunt. Look, it's not that I'm not attracted to you, but I don't like that that was what you were expecting from me tonight. Now, with that being said, I would like to stay and get to know you better, with no strings attached," I sit back down and look him straight in the eyes and ask, "So what happens now?"

"Now we party," he says as he moves into my space. He hesitates for just a second before pulling me in for a kiss. It's gentle at first with his tongue running over my lips until I finally open for him. He takes that as his sign and plunges his tongue deep into my mouth.

I am so fucked.

Backfire

The afternoon festivities involve the public and focus on a pool contest inside the main club bar. My girl's not interested at all in that, so we spend the afternoon outside looking at the entrants in the mini bike show we organized for the ride participants, which she seemed to really enjoy. We also had stalls set up with face painters and shit like that for the kids and a pig roast. You can do an awful lot in the back.

Because the day's activities are pretty much open to the public, we have every member and prospect on alert in case anyone is fool enough to cause trouble in our house. Having all these fuckin' strangers mean we can party, but none of us are getting drunk, well at least not yet.

The clubhouse is closing to the general public at 8pm and I keep Kat pinned to my side while we party into the night. My brothers aren't quite sure what to make of my behavior, giving me odd looks since they've never seen me like this with a woman. Luckily, they've decided to let me be and save the wise cracks for later.

When it's just us and the grounds have been checked, we relax and start to enjoy the night. The back has been cleared of outsiders and people are chilling out there with their drinks. In the main room, an area has been cleared for the ladies to dance and old eighties rock is playing as they begin to let their hair down.

Kat

Lori comes up to Backfire and I and says, "I'm stealing her for a while, big guy. She can't stay by your side all night. Girls have got to have some fun."

With that she drags me onto the dance floor where the women are dancing in a big circle. They make room for us and I start to dance.

"This is Kat," Lori shouts to the group on the dance floor.

We all shout our hello's to each other, but it's too chaotic to get their names. Regardless, they're welcoming me so I go with the flow. After a few more than a few songs, I need a break so I drop out and head to the bar. The prospect behind it hands over a bottle of cider. I'm hot from dancing so I drain it in one go and grab another bottle to keep me going.

Another girl joins me, "I'm Wizz," she says as she too gets some liquid on board. She has short blond hair with pink and purple bits. It suits her. She's taller and slimmer than me, which is no surprise since I'm quite short. She's also dressed in a hippy type top and jeans. "Are you coming back for more?"

I glance at Backfire but he's deep in conversation with Shades and some others so I nod and go back to the girls. It's more fun there anyway.

I can't keep dancing properly because of my ankle so I do the "bottle holder dance." It works for me. I spend the next hour dancing, drinking, and having a giggle with the girls. Even though I don't know them, we seem to be hitting it off rather well, which is a good start. I believe it's possible that I'm a little bit drunk. How did I let that happen? The best course of action is to not question it, just go with it.

Backfire

For all her worry about club life, Kat seems to be having a good time. I had a quick word with Brewer, our VP, and Lori to explain that I may be jumping the gun with my intentions toward her, but I was looking to get to know her more than in the biblical sense. So, when Kat isn't by my side, Lori is looking after her and showing her around. They go off and dance with the other women and Kat seems to fit right in with them. It always helps if a new girl can fit in and hold her own with the others because the last thing we need is petty shit going on between the women. That's never a good thing.

At the end of the night, I have her in my room. I can tell she's tired and she's had enough to drink, but it's not the reason I take her away from the party. During a conversation, she'd innocently made a comment about the cops and about how they're not bothering us about the noise like they do her. I don't know what's going on with that, but I feel pissed off that she's getting fucked with by the cops and I want to know why.

Once I have her alone, I ask her what she meant by it. She tells me that someone is fuckin' harassing her by calling the cops on her when she starts up her bike or turns on her radio. She has no clue who's gunning for her and why they have singled her out. This is what seems to really upset her because she doesn't know what she's done to upset anyone and how far this person is willing to go on with this.

I make a mental note to check into this as she continues to tell me about other things that have been stressing her out like starting her business and how things work differently here than they do in England. I'm not good at this sort of shit, talking so comfortably with a woman like she's doing with me, but I find myself genuinely wanting to hear everything she has to say and try to ease her mind by telling her we can't do much about it tonight, but we'll look into things tomorrow. That shit gets me a huge smile as she sits on my bed and starts to relax. I leave her to take a piss and when I walk back in she's laying there, out cold.

Fuck. Oh well, I suppose I got part of what I wanted—her in my bed tonight.

CHAPTER 6
BREAKFAST AT
BACKFIRE'S

Kat

These aren't my sheets, and these aren't my pillows. This isn't my bed.

Ok, don't panic. THINK!

I open one eye and can't see anyone so I brave it and begin checking for clothes. I'm good. Now that I've established I'm decent, I turn over to look around and there is no one there. I suppose you could say that was anticlimactic.

Backfire's room at the club is a bedroom with an attached bathroom. It's big enough that he can have a small beer fridge and a microwave in one corner and a TV with a shelf of DVD's in another. The bookcase has books on motorcycle engineering, which I would expect, but English, early medieval art history is a bit of a surprise. They're not just quick reads, but serious, in-depth books. I know this because I own them myself. The rest of the wall space has cupboards and a wardrobe. The room is definitely a man's space.

The bathroom door opens and Backfire emerges, luckily with his jeans on, even if they aren't buttoned at the top. The man makes my mouth water. I feel like an idiot as I lie here staring at his well-toned, very tanned chest, but what is even better is the hint of that most interesting V at his hips that could drive any woman mad with lust. He has the perfect amount of body hair with a small trail of it going down below his unbuttoned jeans, along with some very interesting tattoos that I'd love to explore on his chest and back. I'm in lust and I'm not ashamed.

"Morning," I greet him, going for cool.

"Afternoon," he says with a smirk. "There's clean towels in the bathroom and here's some clean clothes for you." I open the plastic bag containing a brand new shirt, a *Support your Local Cycle Devils* tank. The grin on the man's face as he also gives me a pair of knickers with the same Cycle Devils logo has to be seen to be believed. We both get a good chuckle out of the look I give him, but hey, they're clean and new.

"I won't be long," I say, retreating in good order. I'm liking this man more and more. I'm glad he didn't try to kiss me in front of everyone last night. I wouldn't have said no, but I'm not really much for public displays of affection, beyond I think, grinning to myself, being held by him. I take the quickest shower in my life, using his shower gel. I'm not bothered with my hair as I can do that tonight, but the rest of me feels grungy.

I dress quickly and I'm more than slightly amused that the clothes he has given me are the right size. The man knows women. I wonder how good a sign this is.

"Thanks for talking and listening to me last night. I guess I haven't been sleeping well with all the Police and business worries. It must have really helped to just say it out loud because I slept so well, but now I've got to get going soon because I have jobs to do." I say as I prepare to make my way back to my bike.

"Stay a few and at least have breakfast," he practically orders, "I want you to talk to one of my brothers."

I look straight at him, knowing that this is him trying to help me, so I nod as he grins. He gets to keep me for a little bit longer.

Backfire

This girl is challenging me and I find I'm fuckin' enjoying it. She's not clingy and she's independent as fuck. I'm not used to dealing with bitches who have a life and mind of their own and I like this shit. Never thought I'd be bitching one day about getting laid and getting the hell out, then not getting my dick wet but still wanting to hang out the next.

I lead her out through the clubhouse to the dining room where the old ladies have put out a spread for breakfast. The club has an industrial kitchen with all these special pots that keep food warm. It's pretty fuckin' cool in my opinion.

We sort out breakfast for ourselves and I lead her over to the table Trash is sitting at. He gestures for us to join him, looking a little too hard and closely at Kat for my liking.

What the fuck? When did my brothers checkin' out a chick I'm with start to bother me? "This is Kat. She's having cop problems and she's worried about the impact it's gonna have on her business proposal. Think you can help her out?" I say as we sit down.

"What sort of Police problems?" Trash asks.

"The sort that bring them to my door four times in a week for noise issues that vary from starting up my bike to my music," Kat replies quietly, not looking directly at him. I like that she only seems to challenge me. I suppose that's good 'cause I wouldn't want to think that she'd flirt with my brothers.

"Are you thinking of running your business from home?" Trash frowns.

"Not exactly. Because of the recent economic difficulties, they have rezoned an area around the corner from my home into a commercial light industrial area. I want to have my paint shop there and maybe do some of the paperwork from home," she says, this time looking fully at him, but not in the way she looks at me.

"Have you made any sort of application yet?" he says between bites of sausage.

"More of an enquiry than an application," she says between sips of coffee.

"When?"

"The week before last, so the chances are that it could be linked," she replies.

"I'll look into it for you. Where will you be? If you give me your number..."

I am not fuckin' having that shit so I cut in, "I'm taking her home after breakfast so I'll know where she lives."

I feel I've made my point when Kat starts to choke on her eggs at my statement. I can't resist my smile.

Kat

When he takes me to the dining room, it's clean, even after last night's party. The floors have been mopped and the tables wiped down. There are cupboards around the edges and a really smart industrial kitchen is visible through the door.

After I pick out my breakfast from the warming pots, Backfire leads me to a table where one of his brothers sit. His name is Trash, and he looks more like an executive than a biker with his short blond hair and clean-shaven face. He doesn't look soft, nor does he have a heavily muscled body, and his hands don't have a rough, calloused look to them. His nails are clean and evenly trimmed.

Backfire and I tell him the basis of my problems and Trash says he will look into it. As I'm choking over the fact that Backfire will be following me home, Trash grins and says he's a lawyer. I'm so shocked that if I wasn't already choking, I sure as hell would be now.

After breakfast, we get ready to ride. As we go to get on our bikes, Shades pops his head up and says that he'd like to come along for the ride if we didn't mind. Somehow this makes me feel better because in truth, I'm not ready to be alone in my house with Backfire. I know I'm going to cave and it will be very, very soon. I just don't want it to be today so thank fuck for Shades and his intrusiveness.

CHAPTER 7
SUNDAY AT KAT'S HOME

Backfire

What the fuck?

Whoever the fuck is messing with Kat's head is about to learn that she is not alone. As we pull up into her driveway, we see that someone has written the word "WHORE" across her garage door with spray paint.

I look at my girl as she tries to take this all in. Fuck, where did that thought come from? When did she become my girl and not another bitch in a long line of bitches who have been in my bed? She doesn't even fuckin' know that she's the first woman in my forty years to wake up in my bed and we haven't even had sex... Yet.

I go to her and pull her into my arms. I feel her trembling, yet she doesn't say a word; she just holds it all in. Fuckin' good girl. I'll take care of her.

Kat

Fuck, *Fuck*, FUCK.

This shit cannot be happening to me.

Who the hell would do this? I don't even know or bother anyone, so why would someone target me by spray painting *whore* on my garage door? I don't understand, but what I do know is that I need to keep a level head because I have three large, extremely angry men who look like they are ready to tear the neighbourhood apart on my behalf. I just need to stay cool and hope that they follow my lead.

The guys are off their bikes, helmets and jackets strewn out on the drive when, to add to my day, joy of joys, the Police arrive. Backfire and Trash come to my side while Backfire puts his arm around me and Trash greets the officers.

The Police are here for yet another noise complaint. I suppose four Harleys do make a bit of noise, but it's not exactly first thing in the morning and people would have only heard us long enough to get to the driveway, which would be less than a minute at most. I have every right to ride my motorcycle and have friends who come to my home do the same.

Trash points out the paint job to the officers which is obviously hard to miss. That is an actual issue and one that can't be ignored with two Police officers present. He also points out that five visits in seven days is excessive, especially since not one visit has been justified.

Trash mentions words like *victimisation and harassment,* getting their attention.

When the Police have gone, I turn to the guys and ask them in for coffee. I think the whole not drinking and driving belief from England is so ingrained in me that the thought of alcohol and riding doesn't occur to me. It's just the way I am.

The guys follow me in and I put the machine on as they look around.

Backfire asks "You got any garage paint?" I nearly cry at the thought of why he's asking for it but I hold it in and show him the garage. He stomps outside with Shades, which leaves me alone with Trash. In a way, I'm a bit surprised that Backfire left me with another man with the way he has been behaving.

"Don't be surprised," Trash grins reading my thoughts, "He's leaving us to take care of your business. Looks like he thinks your business is his business now."

There is no way I can discuss what's happening between Backfire and myself with anyone else, especially since I'm not sure what exactly is happening, so I shrug my shoulders and say, "Maybe," and go and sort the coffee out.

"Can I have a copy of the enquiry you sent off," Trash asks, "or better yet, can I look at any and all correspondence regarding the business so far?" Smiling, I get everything for him. I can't believe I am getting on this well with a lawyer.

"Will you officially work for me? I could really use all the help you could give me on all of this; the Police, the paint shop, especially as I'm not one hundred percent sure of all the intricacies of Florida law."

Trash smiles, "Of course."

"How does payment work here?"

His expression turns blank and he says, "It's best that we include Backfire in this."

"I met Backfire a week ago for all of a few minutes and I have only hung out with him for a day," I explain to him, "I can't be sure how long whatever this is will last, or even what either one of us expect to happen."

Trash looks me straight in the eyes and says, "I've never seen Backfire treat a woman the way he has you. Don't rush to distance yourself from him."

"I'm not distancing myself. I just moved here a few months ago and I'm just working things out as I go along. I am perfectly comfortable speaking to you about my business with or without him if that's OK with you. I'm the outsider, so I'll follow your lead."

Trash nods his understanding. I don't want there to be any miscommunication as to who he will be working for.

Backfire

When the painting is done, we go back in to a scene of relative peace. Trash is looking through papers as Kat is working in the kitchen with the coffee machine, offering us coffee or pop.

"Have you got any beer, babe?" Shades looks at Kat while I practically growl.

"I don't have any in the house. I don't like it all that much, at least not enough to drink it at home. The only person who comes around regularly is my friend Amber, and she doesn't drink either."

"What do you like?"

"Sweet cider," she smiles, "and not the hot fruit shite drink they call cider here sometimes."

It turns me on when she swears 'cause it seems like it's a rare thing with her, but it shows she has a wild side that I'm just aching to see more of. Fuckin' hell, bitch will have me going around in circles soon.

"I'm going back to the clubhouse now," Trash says as he gets his things together, ready to leave and Shades gets up to go with him. As Trash takes Kat's contact details with him, I give him a look, and all he does is smirk.

Asshole.

At least he's using his trash talking ways to help her. If ever a brother was well named, it's him.

I decide to stay a while longer with Kat. It says something when I don't even mind, knowing that she doesn't have any beer.

"So, Backfire. What do you want to do now?" she asks.

I can't resist the huge smile that breaks out across my face, "Lady's choice."

Kat

"Lady's choice, eh? Well I don't fancy doing the housework that I should be doing, but I feel like a bit of an escape – like a ride to the beach – but to be honest, I think I should stay in and chill out. I wouldn't want anyone to think that their spite has pushed me out of my own house."

"Stay in," he says, "We'll face the assholes together."

"Well if you're staying, would you like the tour?"

He nods as I get up and lead him toward the hall. I give him the grand tour, even the bathrooms, and when I show him the last room, the craft room, I can't help but smile as he takes it in.

"What are you going to do with all this?"

"Some of it will end up in the house. Some of it I'll make into pressies and most of it I will sell at craft markets. It gives me something to do and I enjoy it immensely," I reply.

He nods thoughtfully. He then begins to take more notice of the art on the wall, the trophies in the cabinets, and mostly the tanks I have kept for myself.

"And these?" he gestures.

"Those are tanks I've won awards for. When I set up my business, I plan to put them in cases in the reception area with all the awards. Well, that's what my plans are once this whole mess is figured out."

"Don't worry, Kat. We'll find out what the hell is going on and make shit right," I hope it's sooner, rather than later.

Backfire

Kat is talented; I'll definitely give her that. I'm really impressed with her work and I can't stop myself from wanting to know more about her. She seems smart and has her shit together. She's independent and knows how to take care of herself which is sexy as hell to me, but yet she can go along with things in a way that fits in with the club, even if she doesn't realize that she does so. She's not just some bitch, she's a rare fuckin' find in my world and I'm wanting to stick around and see what could come of this.

As I look around her house, I like what I see. It's not just some meaningless place with a roof over her head; she's made a home for herself that is comfortable and seems to reflect her style. Hell, even I want to come in and take my shoes off, making myself at home. Whatever the fuck it is that she's done, I like it.

We finally get to her bedroom, which has loads of red and gold stuff all over the place, but somehow it doesn't look like cheap or flamboyant. Red seems to be a running theme throughout her home, but there are golds and browns as well—earth colors I guess you would say. This room is what I would consider over the top red, but for some reason it suits her and I can see her here, in this room. It's like she's made a sanctuary; a place just for her.

"You've outdone yourself here. I'm not a bitch, but even I have to admit you've made a nice space for yourself."

"I'm glad you think so. Moving from England to the US alone, I wanted to have a home that feels like home, if that makes sense."

"I get it, Kat. It all suits you from what I've seen of you so far." I decide it's time to get some things out of the way so I start the conversation, "Yesterday, you wanted to leave as soon as you came to the club, but you stayed, even though you had your doubts. What do you think now?" I ask, getting straight to the point.

"The last sort of man I want is a member of an MC, you know that. I'm not looking for something and someone who expects to keep me under some type of lock and key. I live the way I want to live and I have a very big problem with anyone thinking they have a right to tell me I have to do otherwise. Saying that, just from what I've seen up to this point, I like you and your club. I enjoyed myself last night and I'm glad you guys were here to help me today, even though my problems are not yours. So, to answer your question, the only thing I know at this moment is that I want you. What it all means in the long run is sort of beyond me at this point. I don't know what will happen tomorrow, but today – right now – I want you."

"I want you too, Kat. I want you real fuckin' bad," I say, looking her straight in the eyes.

She slowly sits down on the bed, letting me take control of what we both know is about to happen. I'm fuckin' shaking at the thought of being inside this woman.

Kat

Hearing him say that to me has my body on fire. He wants me, but for how long? I don't know the answer to that question, but I'm a big girl and I don't need to read more into this than what it really is. It's just sex.

I watch as he takes me in, somehow seeing my thoughts written all over my face and joins me on the bed. He pulls me into his arms and I'm content to let him just hold me for a moment.

As soon as I let myself relax into him, I start to feel more at ease with my decision to let this happen. This isn't the reaction I expected, but here it is. I've made my decision and I have every intention of following through with it.

I'm sure he can feel the change in my body as I settle down into him. He reaches for my face and tilts it toward his where he begins to glide his fingers gently over my lips. He then reaches down to kiss my forehead, then my nose before finally reaching my lips. At first I don't open my mouth to him, so he just traces his lips and tongue along mine. As I become lost in the feelings he's bringing out of me, I finally open my mouth to him. He's still gentle as his tongue plays with mine, taking what he feels is his. I understand it because I want to give myself to him too.

I know the moment he feels my surrender as he rolls us over so he's lying on top of me, taking some of his weight on his elbows and legs, but letting me feel some of it as he pins me down on the bed. I love this feeling of just letting go and letting someone take control. It's not the way I usually feel or behave, but I don't care at this moment.

I can't hide the evidence of how bad I want this when I hear him growl in my ear, causing my body to jolt up into him and sending chills all over my skin. Feeling completely turned on, I push at him and he rolls off me instantly. He's breathing hard but he quietly watches me, waiting to see what I do next. I pull my boots and socks off. It's not exactly a striptease, but enough for him to know where my head is with this.

Backfire follows my lead and copies my act, then goes a step further and removes his t-shirt. His back has the Cycle Devils' colours tattooed on it. The symbol is of a devil breaking out of a bike wheel. His arms have full sleeves and there are further club tattoos on his chest and legs.

Pulling me back to him, he starts to kiss me as I explore his chest with my hands, feeling his warm skin and the muscle underneath. I sink deeper into the spell he's casting over my body. He begins to raise my shirt up just a bit so his hands are touching the skin around my waist. When he is sure that I'm good with it, he pulls it up over my head and grins when he realises I'm not wearing a bra.

Our hands are everywhere; exploring like a couple of teenagers wanting to feel every part of one another's bodies. Soon we're no longer kissing each other's lips, but using them to further explore other places. This mutual exploring goes on until he reaches my breasts.

When he starts to suck on my nipple, I feel like I could orgasm from that one act alone. He sucks harder and I feel my body tightening up, ready to come when he immediately stops and separates our bodies.

"Last chance to say no," he says. There is no way in hell I will let this stop now.

"I don't need your words, Backfire. I want action, so please don't stop," I beg him with absolutely no shame. He swiftly reaches down to undo my shorts and yanks them down my legs, leaving me naked apart from the Cycle Devils knickers he gave me earlier. The lust in his eyes at the sight of me takes what little self-control I have left from me and like a brazen hussy, I open my legs to him so he can have easy access to my most intimate parts.

"We'll keep these on," he decides. I have no reason to argue. He stands and loosens his belt, unbuttons his jeans and drops them to the floor. Since he's not wearing anything under them, I'm stunned by how big his cock is. He gives me a moment to appreciate what he's working with as I devour every inch of him with my eyes.

I wouldn't change my mind now for anything.

Backfire

As I'm stripping Kat out of her clothes, I clock her tattoos for a later detailed inspection. Instead of girly shit like bright stars and butterflies, she has colored gas tanks and one with a horse and a bike. The others have to wait.

Nothing prepares me for the sight of her, laid out before me in nothing but my club colors on her pussy. It crosses my mind how hot it would be to have my property tat on her there. Fuck, I'm not even inside her yet and I'm imagining claimin' her as mine in my head. I can't believe my train of thought, but she's such a fuckin' sight lying there, waiting for me to fuck her.

My cock is pounding and my balls are aching.

"This first go is going to be quick and hard," I warn her, "just so you know." As I cover my cock with a rubber that I grab from my pocket, I watch as she looks into my eyes.

"Then so be it. I just want you inside of me and I'm tired of waiting," she says.

That's more than I can take. I push a finger deep into her and find her soaking wet. Adding another finger, I find her spot as I push harder into her and she nearly comes apart. I watch her while I work her over and decide I want my fuckin' cock inside of her the first time she gets off with me. I push her panties further to the side and shove myself all the way into her with one hard thrust, causing her to scream out and clench around my cock so tight that I nearly come before I'm even close to being ready. Fuck, she's tight. I just want to lose control with her completely as I pump into her two more times before I feel her come around me. I fuckin' love the sound of her coming around my dick. Fuckin' amazing.

I wanna hear and feel that shit again so I pull her legs onto my shoulders and fuck her harder. I'm gonna do everything I want to her body and she's gonna let me. I'm pulling orgasm after orgasm out of this girl and she's taking as good as I'm givin'. She's giving me all the control and she's enjoying every goddamn second of it.

I switch her onto all fours, ramming even deeper as I pull her long, red hair and watch her back arch as she rides my cock just as hard as I'm thrusting. I swear this woman was made just for me to fuck.

Ramming into her as hard as I can, I can't put off my orgasm any longer so I bend her over with her ass up in the air and take what I need as I come so fucking hard. The best part is she comes at the same fuckin' time, pulling every fuckin' drop out of me with her tight, wet pussy right before she screams my name and collapses.

She just blew my fuckin' mind along with my load, so yeah, I'm keeping her for a while... a long while.

Kat

Backfire took me higher and further than I've ever been before. I lie on the bed, trying to pull myself back together but right now, I can't even move. I hear him moving about the room, dealing with the condom and even cleaning me up before he crawls back into bed with me. Lying on his back, he pulls me to him and settles me where he wants me as weariness sets in and blackness claims me.

I wake up slowly, feeling my body aching in the best way imaginable. I am still lying in Backfire's arms exactly the way I fell asleep and it's the easiest, most satisfying feeling I've ever had.

"Ready for another round?" he asks, feeling me stir in his arms.

I can only nod my head yes, and when I look up at him, he raises an eyebrow at me; he wants my words.

"Yes, I want you to fuck me again, please," I say.

He rolls on top of me and goes to work on my body, but this time he's in no hurry, and neither am I. I really want to play with him too.

Backfire

I'm not fucking Kat, I'm taking my sweet time with her. I'm giving it to her slow, licking and tasting her as she does the same to me. She watches me taste her just as intently as I watch her take me into her mouth, sucking me off and keeping eye contact the entire time. Not only is it intense, it's fuckin' hot as hell, but now I want her tight pussy clamping around me.

I put on a rubber and lay her underneath me. I rub across her already wet clit and push the tip of my cock in. I watch her as her eyes plead with me to move, so I give her what she wants, but slowly. I don't know what the fuck is happening but I want this shit to last just so I can keep touching her, hear her moans and her screams every time she comes for me. This girl has got me feeling shit I don't wanna feel emotionally, but everything I wanna feel and more, physically. I want her, and I want her for more than this.

I let these thoughts drift from my mind as I get back to business as I continue to play with her and give it to her just like this; slow and sweet. We've got lots of time.

CHAPTER 8
BACK TO NORMAL

Kat

Backfire stayed over Sunday night and here it is Monday morning, and he's leaving to go to work.

"So," he says as we drink our morning coffee, "On Saturday, you were wary of being with me, with the club. Where are you now? Because I'll be straight with you, I want to see you again."

"Honestly, I'm more at ease. It's obvious that I like you or I wouldn't have fallen into bed with you. The club ladies I met aren't the downtrodden ones I've met before and your brothers are all great with me. But, after how well last night went, I have to say that I would also like to see you again."

He pulls me in for a coffee-flavoured kiss that would melt any girl's knickers before he leaves. That will certainly hold me over until I see him again—hopefully ruddy soon.

I'm going to put my initial worries about the club aside until I see where this goes. It could just be that we have great sex and eventually go our separate ways so I don't want to prematurely call it quits just yet. If it goes beyond that point, then I'll look long and hard into what I'm willing and not willing to deal with.

Backfire

I catch up with Trash at the clubhouse as Shades and Brewer join us. Trash has his attorney face on and it has me on alert.

"I've contacted one of our cops and got the info on whose been reporting Kat. You won't believe this shit, but it's a councilman named Bob Fish. After doing a little, shall we say, "online research," I looked into the estate that she wants to set her business up on and Fish owns the majority of it, including the property on either side of where Kat intends to open up shop. I started to look into his finances and he doesn't have the money to buy that piece of land on his own. Digging further, I traced the money to a consortium of businessmen. Next I'm going to look into any other properties they control in the area and into the individuals concerned. They are going to challenge Kat's application on the amount of time she's been in the area, noise pollution from the bikes and that she won't be an employer."

"Those are rather sweeping statements," Ace, our President says from behind me. Ace is the perfect fucking pres; a biker through and through but like Trash, he can look at the outside world on its own terms, "And Kat is?"

"Kat is gonna to be my old lady," I say, "she just doesn't know it yet."

At this my brothers fuckin' burst out laughin', just as I damn well knew they would.

"The redhead you were with over the weekend?" Ace asks and I confirm it with a nod.

"Trash has been looking into why the cops are harassing her. Some fucker painted shit on her house and Trash is helping her set up her business. She does custom paintwork," I say with a smile, showing a hint of pride, "and she's fuckin' good at it too."

"How good?" Tinman asks. He's in the fabrication business so this sort of thing would interest him.

"She has loads of fuckin' awards from shows in England and Europe, plus some damn good tanks. That's not me saying it 'cause I'm into her, I'm just tellin' you from what I saw of her work, brother."

Shades and Trash agree with me then Shades pipes up, "The girl's got talent. It's a goddamn shame Backfire found her first," he smirks, grinning smugly, but he stops when my fist finds his gut.

"Seriously, brothers," Ace says quietly, "this situation needs monitoring. If this woman is that important to Backfire and she's inadvertently managed to stir up a hornet's nest, then we'll all deal."

Just like that, Kat has the club's protection, but now to break the news to her of my intentions.

Kat

I get home sometime in the evening from going out to do some research when once again, the Police stop by. Apparently another noise complaint about the loud engine of a bike way too early in the morning. This has gone beyond a joke. I explain to the officers that I didn't go out until 10am and my man left at 9:30am, which is not an unreasonable hour of the day.

As I'm trying to explain how ridiculous these complaints are and how I'm the one who should be complaining over being harassed, the rumble of bikes can be heard in the distance. As they grow closer, I can make out four Harleys coming up the street. I guess this'll be another complaint. As the guys park in my driveway and dismount, Trash comes forward and takes control of the situation, and being so upset and angry, I just leave him to it. Insulting the Police is probably not the way to go. Backfire comes up behind me and puts his arm around my shoulders and I slide my arm around his waist, taking comfort from his support as I breathe him in.

Trash converses briefly with the officers and within no time, they're getting into their patrol car to leave. This is when the guys turn to me. There are two new faces amongst them so I quietly wait for Backfire to introduce me.

"Kat, this is Ace, our President," he says, indicating a handsome man, probably in his fifties, who nods at me. I smile at him and see his eyes light up. Then I'm introduced to the other man, also very handsome, "This is Tinman, our fabricator." This man looks speculatively at me and I get that. A fabricator and a painter usually work professionally well together, so we nod at each other.

"It's nice to meet you both. Please, come on in. I've just gotten home myself so I've nothing prepared, but I can put on a pot of coffee if you'd like."

"We're fine." Ace replies, "We're here to talk about your problems."

That catches me off guard so I stand there just looking at him when Trash interrupts, "We'll use the table."

They settle around the table as Trash pulls out a laptop and paperwork from his backpack. Tinman asks if I have any photos of my work so I reach into a bookcase and bring out my albums. Backfire, Ace, and

Tinman all grab one each and start leafing through them while Trash sets himself up.

"Ok," he begins, "Kat has landed herself in a mess, as evidenced by her regular visitors. Seems she has also set herself up in a competition with a group of rich fuckers out to beat the system and get the land Kat wants to start her business on. So, their plans are to argue how long you've lived in this country, which is a load of crap if you've got the money to set up the business. We can say you're adding to the economy."

"I have the money. I bought this house with cash and I have money in the bank. Housing is cheaper here than in England and the start-up estate is very reasonable, so I can set up and not make a huge profit for the first two years during my start-up period," I reply.

Trash nods and grins, "And there's the noise."

I giggle. What else can I do? "The way the estate is set up, the road access is away from residential areas. Add to that, my work is not like a bike builder. I just get parts delivered in a van so it wouldn't be any noisier than any other unit."

Tinman smiles at me and I know I've made an impression.

"By the way," Tinman says, "I brought you an album of my work to look at if you would be interested. If you would see fit to work with me in the future, I wanted you to see that your work wouldn't be wasted."

"And the final protest is that you will not be an employer," Trash states.

"Well, I suppose initially the paint shop won't be a huge employer. I was going to follow the slow approach and see what happens over a period of time. There is, however, nothing to say that in the fullness of time that there might not be an office worker, another artist, or a general worker sorting out the basics. It all depends, but I would not want to employ people straight out and then fail because I overextended myself or put a person in a job whose role wasn't necessary."

"It sounds like you've got all the answers needed," Ace says, "I believe you'll do."

I automatically look to Backfire, not understanding Ace's statement. When he doesn't give me any hints, I turn to see all four guys smiling at me.

"Have you got any actual work here?" Tinman asks.

Getting that the meeting is over, I smile and show them around. Tinman and the others like the tanks, giving me hope that I have a running start in this market.

I sit down to look at the album that Tinman has brought along to show me as he says, "All the bikes behind the marker are ones Backfire's designed."

Wow. I can see that between the three of us, we could come up with some amazing work. I'm getting more and more excited.

Tinman turns to Trash and asks, "When you looked at that estate, were all the properties taken by this gang?"

"Strangely enough, the guy who put in for one of the larger units withdrew his offer. Why?"

"I need to expand. I'm gonna need more room than what I have now, so if I put in for a unit by my painter, that could benefit both of us."

"Wow," is all I manage to get out. I'm a bit choked up at the thought of potentially having a bloody useful business associate.

"Trash, get an application in for that unit, and let's do it now." Ace orders.

"I need to offload the unit I have now, Boss, to help pay for a new one," Tinman points out.

"No problem. I have a use for the smaller unit so I'll buy yours. Having your application in will take some of the pressure off Kat, stopping these fuckers in their tracks. Going up against an MC, especially one like ours with a huge membership all over the country is a whole different ballgame than trying to pick on a single woman." I know he has directed the last bit at me, and I have to agree with him. Again, it shows me the support I'm getting because of Backfire.

"I'm so grateful that you guys are backing me and helping me out, but I'm a little beside myself as to why? Backfire and I have only just met. Who's to know what we'll be or how long it will last. I don't want to be in a bad situation if whatever is between Backfire and I goes wrong, you understand? What happens if we don't work out?"

"We'll work that out when the time comes," Backfire says.

And that, I suppose, is that.

Backfire

We all head out for dinner and I ride at the back of the group with Kat to the steakhouse the club owns. I left my saddlebags back at her place that hold a small supply of clothes for me and more CDMC panties for her. I also brought some beer.

Kat orders the same as us, another fuckin' point in her favor. She doesn't eat rabbit food and she has no problems joining in on the conversation. Tinman takes a lot of her attention, but when we finish eating, she slides her ass closer to me so we're touching and I like that shit, so I wrap my arm around her shoulders and pull her closer and keep her there as the evening moves along.

After dinner is over, the guys ride with us by Kat's on their way home to make sure that all is ok. Luckily, there's no damage from the front of the house, so they continue on while Kat opens the garage and leaves room for my bike, which lets me know that I'm welcome.

After we secure our bikes and the garage, we walk into the house and Kat collapses on the sofa.

"I've got to admit that this whole thing with your club is a bit overwhelming. I'm happy about it, don't get me wrong, I'm just taken back by how they have jumped in to help me. They don't know anything about me. I'm an outsider, you know?"

"Just accept it, alright. You need the help, me and my brothers are in a position to offer it." I reply.

She lets it go, telling me she'll accept it.

"So, what's in the bags?"

"Beer and clothes."

"I meant to go shopping tonight and grab some things. I wasn't even sure when you'd be back. Are you staying?"

"Brought enough clothes for a few days, babe."

"Fair enough. I haven't unpacked all my clothes so there's an empty cupboard to put your stuff in while you're here. No need to leave your clothes in a bag to get wrinkled."

"Come here," I tell her. She walks into my open arms and I hug her tight, "I appreciate that, babe. I find myself enjoying your company, and I'm hopin' you might feel the same way. I like the idea of seeing where this could go, and you're the first woman I've even considered such a thing with."

"I like that idea too. I'm not looking to rush into anything, but I like you too so let's just enjoy the ride, ok?" Then she looks down at my bag, "Do you want to put the beer in the fridge?"

"Yeah, babe. I'll do that now."

CHAPTER 9

PANIC

Kat

It occurs to me in the middle of the night that I have just met a man that I have taken up with rather quickly. I'm nervous that it's all moving rather fast. Why would I offer up a cupboard for his clothes? It didn't occur to me how it sounded until after I had said it. I hope he takes it for what it is; a place to put his clothes for the next few days while he's here and not like I'm offering him space in my home. We know nothing of one another really, and I want to take my time getting to know him.

Last week I was crowing about how clever and independent I am, and now I'm curled up naked in bed with a man whose real name I don't even know. I only know he's part of an MC and that he makes custom bikes. Does he have any ex-wives? Does he have any kids? Would I be ok with any of that?

I NEED TO GET A GRIP.

I'm in lust. Except for those issues that may or may not be, it seems he's everything I want. He even has friends who are willing to help in matters I'm not sure I could handle on my own, but he's in an MC, and that could mean he's possibly even killed before.

My mind starts to go places I really don't need it to go and I start to shake as the implications of my stupidity catch up with me in the dark, causing Backfire to wake up.

"What's your name?" I demand.

"Babe, what time is it?"

"Three o'clock. What the fuck's your name?"

At this he sits up and flicks the light on. Even in his sleep filled haze, he must see how I'm feeling by the look on my face, which I can only imagine as freaked out and scared as he comes toward me slow and easy, like he might scare me away with one wrong move. At this moment, I can't say that he would be wrong in that assumption, either.

Backfire

Fuck me. My girl's eyes are wild and terrified. I don't know if it's me or a bad dream that's brought this shit on so I best take this slow.

"My name is Sean O'Connor. You know I design the bikes that Tinman makes. I don't have much of a story to tell you about myself and I think you're freaking out over how fast you see us moving, am I right? Is that what this is about?" She nods her head yes, so I continue, "If you think this is scary for you, imagine how I feel. I don't do this shit, babe. I get what I need and I get gone, but I'm so tired of that kinda life. Seeing you so independent and sure of yourself is a big turn on for me, but it's also something I don't see with any of the women I've been around. I like that shit about you. I hope like fuck this continues with us. I have no baggage to carry into a relationship and all I really want is to ride this wave and see where it takes us. It doesn't matter how long we've known each other, Kat, it's how you feel about it that matters. I think this is worth a try. Every relationship starts somewhere, right?" As I say this I feel my balls shriveling up into tiny raisins. Last week all I wanted from a woman was my cock in a hole, I didn't fuckin' care which, didn't fuckin' care whose, as long as it was there when I wanted and gone when I was done.

What the fuck is happenin' to me?

While I'm considering my new girly behavior, I see her start to relax and calm down.

"Can we go back to sleep now, babe? I have work in the morning."

She nods slowly, lookin' less and less spooked by the minute. I look her in the eyes as I lower myself back down on the bed, knockin' the light off as I do. I have my arms open to her so she can come to me if she wants to, and after a moment, I feel her slowly move into me, taking the comfort I offer as we slowly drift off into a peaceful sleep.

When we wake up the next morning, I know Kat is pissed at herself for what happened during the night, and in a way, so am I. I'm not pissed that she woke up feeling the need for a little self-preservation; I get that. I'm pissed that I've pushed this shit too quickly, not giving either one of us time to even draw a fuckin' breath.

She comes out of the bathroom looking sheepish. Fuck, I know how we deal with this is actually far more important to us as a couple than how good we are at sex. Us? Shit.

I lift my hand out to her and she comes to me, eyes downcast. I take us to the living room, the bed isn't the place for this, and I sit us on the sofa.

"I've made a mess of this. I was congratulating myself on being clever until I let my brain catch up only to realize that I didn't know anything about you and sort of panicked."

"Yeah, I got that, so let's work on learning things about each other. Like I said, this shit is all new for me too, and I guess knowing each other is a pretty damn important factor. I wanted you so bad that I didn't give a shit about covering the basics. Bottom line, we learn about each other together."

"Yeah, I get that," she smiles, "I can't believe I didn't ask you before. When I woke up and realised I didn't know your name I totally freaked. I'm sort of over it now."

"With the speed things are happening between us, I imagine there'll be other times when you'll question shit about me. All I ask is that you always come and talk to me about whatever is on your mind," I tell her. "Is there anything you want to ask me now?"

"Well, now that you mention it, I wonder if you can tell me more about your club."

"Why don't we start with what you know about MC's. What are your experiences with them over in England?"

"Well, an MC is an outlaw club; one percenters. We also have clubs in England known worldwide like the Hell's Angels who fit into that category. Then there are Motor Cycle Clubs, MCCs, who are not outlaw, but more like a riding club is here. MAG, or Motorcycle Action Group, HOG (Harley Owners Group), which you have here also. Really it's just about the same with a few slightly different terms."

"That sounds about right, and you understand that a one percenter is not necessarily a member of an organized crime family? You understand that it's just a bike club outside the "normal" guidelines."

"Oh yes," she says, "I've been around MC's enough in the UK to know that it's not completely like what you see on TV."

"Yeah, that's a fuckin' good way of sayin' it. There are criminals in all walks of life and there are good guys just the same. Also, not every cop is bent, just some."

She bursts out laughing.

"Fair enough. And if I look online into the Cycle Devils, will I find crime associated with your club's name?"

"You'll find a brother or two has been arrested for assault, even drunkenness and possession, but not all of us."

Kat puts her head to one side, a sign I'm noticing she gives when she's deep in thought. After a few minutes tick by, she looks like she's come to some sort of decision and says, "I can live with that."

Then she smiles as she jumps to her feet and heads to the kitchen, "How about some breakfast?"

Then just like that, things between us are fuckin' worked out. Being with Kat is both easier and harder than I thought it would be, but I'm seeing that when it's easy, it's fuckin' perfect.

Kat

The next morning I go for a ride. Being out on the road, my mind starts to clear. A ride works for me every time. I am well over my meltdown and ruddy pleased that Backfire is still planning to be around after it.

We arranged to meet up after work outside a local supermarket where he'll be bringing his truck. It feels simple; nothing too heavy. I need food in my house and he plans to help me eat some of that food so this is simple and comfortable. I don't imagine that this will occur a lot, but it'll be good to know what he likes and compare it to what I like.

I haven't told him that I picked this supermarket because they have an English food section, but he'll soon learn. I also haven't told him that I use a local butcher and a greengrocer for a lot of my fresh stuff. Going to different shops doesn't seem to be how many Americans shop, but it works for me. I prefer variety and like to make my own choices.

When the time came to shop, I found that I was actually having fun. Who expects food shopping with a man to be fun? He doesn't even whinge when he's faced with the prospect of going to more than one shop to buy stuff, though he admits he's never tried it before. The only issue we had was when it was time to pay. He wanted to pay for it all. His argument was that I had just bought my house, but even when I offered to go halves, he said yes, but only if I sold him half the house. Have you ever noticed how it's always ruddy money that causes most fights? I swear, men.

Backfire

What the fuck is Marmite and why am I shellin' out five bucks for a jar of it? This store has a whole aisle of British stuff, which looks nothing like food, and why does the mustard come in such a small tube? Kat just smiles and says I'll find out, but it stays firmly in the shopping cart.

After everything else, she tries to pay. I am so not having that shit. The look on her face when I picked her up and put her behind me at the checkout counter was fuckin' funny though.

The best part about it is she clamps her mouth shut and saves that shit for later when we're alone. That's my girl.

It suddenly occurs to me that I haven't given her those panties. I stuffed them in a drawer with my stuff, probably because I wanted to get my stuff in that drawer quick before she changed her mind. I think the right moment to give her a pair will be if she starts trying to talk money with me at home.

What the fuck? When did her house become home?

Once we make it back to her house, she unpacks the groceries and puts them away, all while cooking dinner at the same time. Stupid things like today are teaching me a lot about her. I decide to not go too heavy on the money front for a while, see how things pan out for us.

As she cooks, I go and check the bikes out. I'm not surprised to see hers is well maintained, adding another point in her favor. Looking around the garage, I see a load of insect netting. I'm gonna assume she's planning to enclose the backyard. Interesting.

I go back into the house and through to the yard as Kat follows me out.

"I plan on making this area here into a barbecue and gathering spot. I want to make that area grassy and over there, I want to put one of those above ground swimming pools. That's part of why I bought this house. There was potential for the outdoor space I needed."

"Sounds like a fuckin' good plan. I'll help you with it."

Kat takes my declaration in stride, "That would be cool. I'm still learning all the hazards of the area so it would be a real help to have someone who knows the local wildlife and how to deter it. So far, I've had a possum in the yard whose bite is apparently pretty painful, and a snake in the kitchen. That was a massive reality check for me about where I am now."

"What sort of snake?"

"A scary one. Snakes belong in a zoo. I phoned a man to get rid of it and didn't really want to know anything beyond that."

Guess my girl isn't into everything that Florida has to offer.

After a chill sort of evening, we fall into bed. The sex is soft and gentle and I take my time, savoring every second of it with her. This was so much more than fucking. This kind of sex is new to me but with Kat, it's like I'm feeling all kinds of shit I never felt before. I just relax and fuckin' enjoy it. I can see myself getting used to this permanently.

CHAPTER 10
ONE MONTH LATER
BABY STEPS

Kat

I had Marmite on toast for brekkie, which is something that Sean is not impressed with. It's fine with me. It just leaves more for me. You either love it or you hate it, and I'm guessing he's never going to be a fan. It is, however, good for a giggle to offer it to him to watch his face. He really can't hide his dislike for it, which is rare for him because he can do "lack of expression" all too well.

The last month has been amazing. Sean spends a lot of his time here when he's not working or doing things with the club and I can't say that it's been awful, especially for someone like me who enjoys having my own space. We move around each other with ease. It feels like a dance that we've always done, making everything feel comfortable and smooth.

I don't think that Backfire will ever truly get that I don't want to be buried in his club. I still want my own life away from it all. It looks like part of my work life is going to include them so I want to keep a few things separate because it's all just so new and I'm already set in my ways.

Since it's Wednesday, I'm getting ready for craft night. Tonight is special because Lori is coming for the first time. It's a big deal in my head to include someone that is part of the club to my home when Backfire isn't here, but over the last month, I've started to get to know her better and I like her, so I'm giving it a go. If it works out, there are a couple more of the old ladies I think I could like. I've taken special care getting ready and done some baking, even though Amber is the Cookie Queen and is sure to bring loads of different sorts. I've been out and got a book on making non-alcoholic cocktails and the stuff to make them to play with tonight, because how can that go wrong?

The Cycle Devils always have a members-only club night on Wednesday, which couldn't have worked out any better for me and my crafting night.

To make some money to pay for holidays and things like that, I plan to make bits to sell at the craft fair in St. Petersburg. I'm really looking forward to it because I know it'll be fun.

Amber and I plan to share a stall as she does all sorts of different things than I do. I am an artist first, but I can knit well enough to sell things, which is really useful in Florida where woolly hats are de rigueur, so I started to knit wire jewellery instead.

Amber is the first to arrive. As soon as she walks in the door, Backfire comes up behind me, putting his arm around my waist in his claiming gesture. It seems to be his thing in front of everyone. Amber just smiles, being used to this by now. Thank fuck for that.

"You can stop with your claim. I have no intentions of taking her from you," she says and they both begin to laugh.

Just then I hear two HD's approaching. Clearly they're coming here, but he looks out to check anyway.

"Brewer and Lori," he says. "I'll go to club night with Brewer and we'll be back here for Lori later."

"Ok," I say as Brewer and Lori walk in. They say their hellos to Amber and then the guys get ready to go. Backfire pulls me into his arms at the same time Brewer embraces Lori but I'm too busy kissing him to notice anything else going on around me.

After the guys leave, our little crafting party begins. The snacks and goodies are on the kitchen counter while our crafts are spread out all over the table.

"Let's play," I begin, "Lori, do you do any crafting?"

"I crochet," she says, diving into her backpack and bringing out some stunning work; an amazing traditional tablecloth and the cutest little Santa Chrissy deccies.

"I tend to make the decorations throughout the year to sell them at Christmas," she explains, "If I leave it until then, I can't meet the demand."

"They're awesome," Amber says, "I'd like to make some."

"Strange that you should say that," Lori smiles, "I brought some hooks and extra wool."

We play at making ourselves some cocktails then begin our night, making little Santa's. I'm not the best crocheter in the world, but even I start to get the hang of it and I find I really enjoy it. Amber and Lori are obviously much better at it than I am, but I'm learning.

Eventually our conversation turns to bikes and the club. I talk to Lori, trying to get a feel for how I'll get on with the girls at the club, or if they will even accept me, while Amber plays Mother Hen a bit and wants to make sure I'm going to be safe.

"Okay," Lori says, "Let's talk about bikes. Kat, you've obviously ridden bikes for a while. Do you ride, Amber?"

"No. I've thought about it, but to be honest, the snowbirds put me off. Some of their driving is abysmal, and I feel safer in a car."

"There is always a trike. You'd definitely be safer on one of those," Lori points out. I'm a bit shocked because I thought that Amber didn't ride because she didn't want to, not that she had a reason.

I feel like a bad friend, so when a girl feels off, you just have to go for the obvious remedy, "Anyone for dessert?"

Backfire

Ace starts our meeting by getting the normal officer's reports. The officers are Brewer, our Vice President. Bullet is our Sergeant at Arms. Tex is our Road Chief and OB is Treasurer. All have nothing to report, except OB does bring up that he hasn't gotten all the money owed in yet for the ride, and that he'll give us a final total by next week when everything is sorted.

Ace continues the meeting by briefly informing everyone of Kat and her situation, making it very clear that we are supporting her.

Shades says, "Sock and I had a few words with Mr. Fish at the time. Backfire's confirmed that this has resulted in no cop problems for her since their last visit a month ago."

Trash adds, "I've applied for all the properties that the association doesn't own and informed them of the fact. With any luck, they'll realize that Kat is the least of their fuckin' worries."

I formally tell my brothers, "Just so you all know, Kat is mine. In front of my brothers here, I want to acknowledge that I intend to make her my old lady." They laugh and torment me, just like I fuckin' knew they would. Still, her being mine makes her part of the club and these guys would literally kill to protect her.

It's strange, but it feels good—taking that step that to me declares her as mine. Maybe one day I'll go the whole hog and give her my property patch. I know my brothers would be a lot happier if I do this after I've known her longer, not that they'll get in my face about it, but they come first. Hell, some of them haven't even met her yet.

The agreement to help her is partly because her work can help club brothers' businesses and partly to help me. The guys who have met her like her well enough, but wouldn't have gone this far to help her if it wasn't for me. That's part of the benefit of being in a club; my brothers look out for me and mine.

Kat

We are having a blast. We're all getting on, making some good stuff too.

Amber and I are picking Lori's brain. I need to know a little more about life with the Cycle Devils as a woman, and Amber is interested because she is my friend and wants to support me.

Lori tells us that the club has many chapters across the East Coast. They also have chapters in Germany and are in discussions with a club in England about patching over. It's a big club with a lot of internal and external support. The West Florida chapter is made up of a combination of brothers who have their own business skills. Some are even brothers who have moved to Florida after they retired. It makes for a very impressive charter as these retired members bring with them years of experience.

Lori also tells us what I'm beginning to work out for myself; the club has no problem with letting their women live the way they want to live. The men don't try to rule over their women, which makes me feel so much better about my relationship with Backfire.

Lori is also excited about my tanks. She comes up with the idea of making a shopping trip, specifically to hit up shops that may be useful to me as possible sales venues so we agree to go tomorrow. Amber can't come, but in all fairness, she agrees that mooching around a load of biker type shops is not her cup of tea. At least she likes tea.

CHAPTER 11

SHOPPING WITH LORI

Kat

So Lori and I set out on our shopping trip at the biker-style shops. We decide to leave our motorcycles in my garage and take the car, just in case we leave with more than our bikes can handle.

We figure on having a look around the sort of establishments where I could entertain myself and maybe think about going into business with; bike shops, clothing shops, tattooists, that sort of thing. It never hurts to know who sells what, especially when you want to merge into the local scene.

After some basic research into the local biker amenities, I had come up with a load of places I wanted to check out. There are actually a lot of places to try. No real surprise there with the amount of potential income from all the tourists. There are a few premium name, bike suppliers and a few local small businesses, but no custom paint workshops. That is my in.

The Harley Dealership was a blast. Loads of bikers are hanging about and the shop has the biggest selection of t-shirts and merchandise I have ever seen. We even got asked to play some pool. I lost, of course. I really am rubbish at pool, but Lori kicked ass.

The local leather shop was also my kind of place. First off, I love the smell of leather. Then there's the fact that I'm well into the cowgirl/biker look. Any leather with fringe and tassels, I'm your girl. I get myself a western-style, brown waistcoat and make a list of future things in my little head for further purchase because a girl can't have too much leather.

Then I see my favourite type of shop—a Christmas shop. It doesn't have to be anywhere near December for me to love these, and it's really time to buy something new for my new house so I pop in and find a new Harley decoration for my tree. There are also some wicked western horse type ornaments that just have to be purchased. Lori is as bad as me, well actually, she's worse. She admits to having the whole outdoor decoration thing at her house every year.

It's really good to know that Lori and I get along so well. She's going to introduce me soon to other old ladies in the club, so we'll see how that goes, and I'm hoping it will go extremely well.

CHAPTER 12

A DISASTROUS MEETING

Kat

"Backfire, do you realise the Police haven't been around for a month?"

"I don't reckon they'll be back again," he smirks.

"Why?"

"A couple of the guys had a word with the fucker who was complaining, helping him to see the error of his ways," he laughs.

Not sure if that will be a good or bad thing, I'll go for good, hoping that the problem is solved. I'm just a little irritated at the fact that he knew about this and didn't see fit to tell me what was happening. Best I venture carefully here.

"I appreciate it, I really do, but is there anything else I should know? Is there anything else that you guys have done for me that I need to be aware of?"

"This and that. Nothing for you to be concerned about, though. It's my job to look after things while we're together so you don't have to worry."

Now how do I reply to that without offending him? It appears that he honestly believes that he's responsible for sorting out my problems when I'm the one who needs to worry about them, but I'm going to let it go for now. I understand what he's doing and with us being so new, I don't want to turn this into an argument. I know that it will have to be a series of subtle conversations for another day. I'm also pretty sure that telling him we need rules is not going to be a popular move. I feel the need to think about this through before having the discussion.

I tell him I have an appointment to go to today, not going into the details of it though. It's with a local councillor in regards to my business start-up application. While I don't often wear dresses, I am prepared to wear a pair of proper trousers and a smart blouse. I'm even using the car and not the bike.

The meeting is at the unit and the councillor introduces himself as Bob Fish. We are discussing my plans for the future one minute and then the next, someone has grabbed me from behind and clasped a smelly hand over my mouth and nose. As I fall unconscious, I know that Backfire is going to be pissed at me. Stupid, stupid girl, thinking I was proving a point.

Backfire

Kat's been gone for ages; far longer than I fuckin' expected, which has me starting to worry about her. I do not like this feeling. What the fuck?

Kat

I come around and survey my surroundings. How fucking fantastic is this? It appears that I'm locked in a room of a vacant house. On the plus side, I'm not tied up, but that's the only plus. I need to work out how to get out of here.

First thing I notice is that I must be near water because there are those huge bugs —palmetto bugs.

There should be a law about insects being so big. I stand quietly for a while, just listening. When I hear nothing that relates to human activity, I decide to have a go at kicking the door in. After all, what's the worst that can happen?

All those Tae Kwon Do lessons seem to have paid off because once I deliver a turning kick to the door and voila! The door breaks open. I assume it must have been a bit rotted already, but I'm not complaining. Looking around the hallway, all I can really see are boarded up windows and insect things that I don't want to see. Looking at the front and back doors as opposed to the windows, I decide that the windows look the least secure. I start to kick through the planking. I knew all that breaking practice would come in handy someday.

It doesn't take long to break enough wood for me to get through the obstruction. After that, it's relatively easy to get out of here. My suggestion to any kidnapper would be not to leave someone alone in a house with big, flying bugs.

Once I'm free of the bug house, I start to walk. The last thing I need is for my idiot kidnappers to drive past me, especially as I have no idea what car or van they have, or how many people there are. I'm trying to hang around the side roads, which also doesn't help because so few people walk, especially dressed like this, even if I do look a tad shabby. There is even the possibility that I could walk straight past the kidnapper's house.

Giving up on the side roads, I decide it'll be easier to dodge and hide if I go on the main roads where there are shops and bars to potentially dive into. It's also so much easier to work out where I'm at on the grid to work out how to get home.

I never imagined that I would ever be kidnapped, but if I did, this really isn't what I would think it would be like. Where the fuck is my handsome rescuer, or even Backfire? Seriously though, what did they plan to accomplish by just leaving me there with plenty of options of getting away. Total amateurs in my educated opinion.

Even though I look a sight, I decide to carry on, I've worked out where I am and I'm heading in the right direction. I start to wonder if it's even safe to go home. They would obviously have access to my address and my bag with the house key in it, so where do I go?

I know how to get to the Cycle Devils and to Amber's from here. It's possible that the kidnappers know there is a link between me and the club, and they'll exploit that to try to take me again. Amber's house it has to be, so I continue walking until I get there. It's getting dark now, which somehow makes me feel safer. There's less possibility of being spotted. Let's just ignore the potential risk from any other type of criminal; one disaster at a time. Thank Heaven I used to do a lot of walking in England. Although the weather here for exercise is awful, at least the terrain is easy.

Amber opens the door and the look on her face is priceless. "Please," I say, "Can I have a bath first and give you an explanation later?"

"Of course!" She has a job to do, which helps as she focuses on that, which gives me a moment's respite. "Do you want a drink? Are you hungry?"

"Oh God, yes, can I use your phone?"

"Help yourself to anything you want and I'll make you something to eat while you're having your bath. I'll sort you out some clothes, too."

"Thank you."

Backfire

Kat has been missing all day and it's now late evening. I'm really fuckin' worried. I called in the guys and Trash found a report of her car, burned out on the wrong side of town. I have no clue as to why she would have gone there. Trash is hacking into her emails but it seems to be taking forever. I know she's not home and there's no one at her house. I don't actually have a key to see if there's anything lying around to help give me any clues as to where she could be. I'll break in if I have to.

My phone starts to ring and I don't recognize the number. This doesn't help my mood.

"Yeah," I bark.

"Backfire?" comes Kat's hesitant voice.

"Where are you?" I reply, far nicer than I was a second ago.

"Amber's," she replies.

"What's the address?" she rattles it off quickly, "Don't move. I'll be there in fifteen."

"I hate to ask this, but could you please bring me a pair of knickers, er, panties?"

This request halts me in my tracks, "Yeah, babe," I reply softly now, "I won't be long."

Kat

I take a few minutes to settle myself down. Backfire will be here soon and I need to collect my thoughts.

I hear the sound of Harleys approaching and as soon as they make it to the door, I fling myself into Backfire's arms. He wraps me up tight and I instantly feel comforted until he growls, "What the fuck, babe?"

"I do believe I was kidnapped." I reply, going for blasé, but hearing the sounds coming from the guys behind Backfire, I figure I failed.

"Explain. Now!" Ace orders.

"I was contacted by the council regarding the application for my unit, so I met the councillor and ended up locked in an insect infested house – which I seriously disliked – so I escaped. I wasn't sure where to go that was safe from the Bugmen, but thought Amber was my best option and I called you as soon as I got here."

"What was the name of the councilman you met with?" Ace asks.

"Bob Fish." I reply. The guys continue to snort and growl, while Backfire simply holds me.

"What the fuck did you think you were doing?" he demands.

"Meeting the Council to press forward with my application." I reply, being positively reasonable to him under the circumstances.

"He's bent, Kat," Backfire snarls.

"Well I know that now," I say, still going for calm, "The question appears to be when did you? Was it before I got drugged, kidnapped and locked up with huge fucking bugs? Bugs that fly? Was it before I had to rescue myself and walk for miles, in fear of being taken again? Was it before I was scared to go to my own home?" Ok, now I'm losing it.

I look at the guys and realise they all knew, and no one bothered to tell me. Amber realises it too and orders the miserable fuckers from her house. They don't seem to want to go, but Amber threatens them with the Police. By the look on her face and the sound in her voice, I'm pretty sure they get that she will do it, MC be damned.

"Amber, honey. Can I crash here for the night?"

"Sure you can. You're always welcome here."

I kiss her cheek and drag my weary ass to bed, too angry at first to sleep, but I also should have known better.

CHAPTER 13
KEEP CALM AND CARRY ON

Kat

As I expected, I didn't exactly sleep well last night. Strange day, strange bed, and most strange of all, I'm missing Backfire. I knew I was into him but I've become attached to the man. This is so not good.

I honestly don't know what to do. I'm crazy about this man, ignoring years of knowing better than to be with a bloke in a club. I know he and his brothers have done nothing but try to help me, but it also appears that they were keeping things that affected me to themselves, surely thinking they were "protecting me." If I had known that any council members were involved in what was happening, I would most certainly have been a lot more careful about meeting a councillor, even if I wasn't aware of his name until the meeting.

I confess I am seriously PEEVED.

I am so used to looking after myself. The fact that my new bloke has been keeping things from me that have actually endangered me pisses me right off.

The obvious answer to me is to be finished with him, yet there is a part of me that doesn't want to be. I fancy the pants off him and want to build a life with him. If I'm truly being honest, I don't want to part with the hot sex. He is amazing in bed.

Finally, and most surprisingly, a part of me likes his brothers. Trash has been so helpful and Tinman, I could easily see working with. Shades is sort of like the little brother you love to hate. Lori and I could be really good friends very easily. Then there are loads of other guys and their ladies who I'm just starting to know, but even if I don't know their names, they all smile and nod at me. Surely that's not something to be sneezed at.

Bottom line, Backfire and the club withheld important shit from me that was about me. Don't they see what keeping this from me has done? If I would have known any of this, I would have been more watchful and I certainly would not have gone to that meeting alone. These guys are obviously not afraid of the Cycle Devils if they kidnapped me, even though they didn't do a very good job. But if they did, where would I be now? I was lucky they did a shit job of it, that's for sure.

Can I trust him after this?

Can I be with a man I don't trust?

I need chocolate, but only the English stuff will do.

I'm so pissed at myself for putting aside my ideals because I wanted Backfire, and even after everything that's happened, I still do.

Backfire

Shades and I are still outside Kat's house when she gets home. We made sure it was secure last night. Since her house keys are gone, we had to get new locks on her doors. We also dealt with her burned out car as best we could without her and now there is a loaner in the driveway for her in case she needs it. I can't believe how hard it is to face her now after last night. An omission on my part caused her to suffer, and things could have been so much worse. She has every right to be pissed, and I have no clue as to how the fuck to make it up to her.

Amber drops her off on her way to work. Kat looks rough, shattered even. It's obvious she sees us but she's trying to ignore us. I feel like I've been kicked in the gut. I want this woman with every fiber of my being, and now I fucked up so bad, she won't even acknowledge me standing here. I just want to make this shit right.

Kat

Backfire is waiting for me. He's obviously been working at fixing things because I now have a car sitting in the drive and I know he has checked the house and changed the locks because I see a new door handle.

What the hell do I say to him?

I decide to look at him and I can tell that he is just as unhappy as I am. He's holding himself in check, leaving the decision of breaking our silence up to me.

I don't waste any time thinking about it. I run into his arms and he wraps himself around me. My anger diffuses once I feel his warm and tight embrace, telling me he feels just as I do. We don't speak. We just stand here, taking comfort in each other.

Eventually we draw apart. He takes my hand, leads me to the door and produces a new key to the new lock.

"We had to have all your locks changed."

I nod my head in understanding, too tired to do anything else. I hear a Harley start up and turn to wave at Shades as he leaves us alone.

"Are you hungry?" I ask.

He shakes his head, "All I want to do is go to bed." He stands there silent for a moment, looking at the floor like he's trying to find a way to say what is on his mind, "It's my fuckin' fault," he mutters, looking me straight in the eyes. "I didn't realize there was a threat to you and you got hurt 'cause of me. I don't feel like sorry is even a strong enough word for what I want to say. I don't expect you to forgive me, but please, just let me hang with you until everything is sorted then I'll fuckin' go and leave your life in peace. I don't want to lose you, babe, but I just want to stay for now to keep you safe."

Shit. I am still seriously pissed about the whole situation, but when a strong, proud man like Backfire bares his heart and soul to you, you'd be one hell of a stupid woman to hold things against him. I don't want to be stupid, so I reach out to him and settle my head under his chin. After a second, I feel him wrap his arms around me and feel him repeatedly swallow. Maybe it's tears, but I don't need to know. We stand together for a timeless moment soaking each other in.

"Alright then," he says as he begins to pull me with him to the bedroom. "Shower?" he asks. I nod and he begins to strip off his clothes. He then comes to me and does the same, taking care of me. Once we make our way into the bathroom, he starts the water and waits for it to reach the perfect temperature before we both make our way inside the stall. We're still quiet, but we both start to relax as the hot water seeps into our tired muscles.

We wash each other. The feel of his skin under my hands and his hands soothing my body relaxes me further. There is no doubt in my mind that this man's comfort is what I need now. We can sort the details out later.

We dry each other after the shower and go straight to the bed where he slowly begins to kiss me. In that moment, I understand that this man is more to me than principles, which are all very well, but they don't keep you company and warm at night. I bite back my problems until later when we can have a proper talk and allow myself to wallow in the comfort that he is offering, like a warm blanket on a cold night.

Backfire

Things aren't as bad as I thought with Kat, and I thank fuck for that. I feel her relax into me and it feels like a wall breaks down between us. It's fuckin' fantastic.

This time, all I want is for Kat and me to connect even more. There is something between us already and I want to reinforce that; make it stronger. I want her and I'm about to make sure I've branded myself onto her, inside and out. I don't want to fuck her or be rough, but what I want to do is make love to her to prove that she's mine.

I take control of her mouth and kiss her 'til she's breathless, all the while my hands are squeezing her tits and rolling her nipples between my fingers. I'm touching her everywhere from her face, her stomach, her ass—wrapping her legs around my waist, rubbing my cock along her clit while I begin sucking her tits, making her moan and pant out my name.

I can feel her nipples harden so I begin to suck harder, adding little bites and harder pulls. At this point she's gasping, begging me to take her so I put her on her back and with one smooth thrust, I'm in so deep my balls smack her ass. Since getting our tests taken care of, I love that I get to take her bare; no more condoms. It's just me, her, and nothing in between. I don't go slow and I don't go fast, but I go deep. I'm claiming her as mine. She needs to get this. With every stroke, she rocks back against me. I watch her body as she moves with mine and it's fuckin' hot as hell. It doesn't take long before she's screaming with her release and I come the minute her walls tighten around me. We continue to move even after we're spent. I want to stay inside her like this forever, so I keep going 'til I'm hard again, making her come for me over and over while giving it to her slow, then rough. I'm not even close to being done claiming her, so we're both looking at a very long morning.

CHAPTER 14
GUN CULTURE

Kat

Backfire and I had crashed after a morning of extreme sex. There is no other way to describe it. When we both had come multiple times, we curled up together and he wrapped his arms around me. Safe in his arms, I fell asleep.

We get up at midday, and as I begin making brunch, he comes in behind me.

"Babe, not to ruin the mood or anything, but I need to ask you if you have a license to carry a concealed handgun?"

"I have no idea how to use a gun." I answer him.

"What?" he appears shocked. I giggle. Americans are so used to their gun culture. The idea that other societies don't have guns sometimes shocks them. "You don't own a gun?"

"Nope. I never could afford the expense of joining a gun club, and that's the only way to use a handgun in England. It's illegal to own them and even if you did, the hoops you'd have to jump through didn't seem worth it. Actually, it's never even occurred to me to get a gun. I've only occasionally thought about learning to use one when I saw shooting competitions at big sporting events on the telly."

"Then why don't you and I go to the shooting range this weekend as a bit of an introduction."

"Like a date?" I ask.

Grinning, he just shakes his head at me, "After what happened yesterday, I want to increase security around you and my brothers agree. At least one of us will be with you at all times, and this weekend I will be your personal bodyguard. That means you've got me day and night, babe."

"I'm sure I'll cope with this impending disaster," I giggle and push myself into his arms. "So tell me," I say hoping to catch him a little off guard, "whose brilliant idea was it to not tell me all the relevant information about the Fishie Man?"

Backfire

"I honestly don't think it was a decision to tell you or not. It just never occurred to me 'cause I assumed it was handled. Looking back now, I can see that was wrong. At the time, I just thought I was protecting you. It was Bob Fish that was reporting you to the cops. We had a little chat with him and there was no more issues, so I just thought the matter was done, even though we thought there was also a strong connection between Fish and the association trying to buy up that whole industrial park."

She is quiet while she digests what I have to say.

"I fucked up, babe. I didn't realize there was a physical threat to you. I thought everything had been sorted out." I can't express how I feel that my actions caused her to suffer. "I don't want anything else to happen to you." At this she raises her hand to touch

my cheek and buries herself even more into my arms.
Fuck, I'll take it.

CHAPTER 15
LIKE IN THE MOVIES...

Kat

Once evening arrives, we head out to the clubhouse together. I had thought about going on the back of his bike, not his custom, which is a hardtail, but his 'everyday' bike, which is a standard Harley with a pillion seat (a 'bitch pad', he calls it), but my stupid legs hurt from all the exercise yesterday. I had given up proper Tae Kwon Do training because of my ankle, but it seems years of drill work up and down the hall, repeating kick after kick had stuck in my muscle memory. It turned out to be a really useful skill to have, but it doesn't feel that way today.

The only problem with going on the back of his bike is that the leg position looks even more uncomfortable than riding my own. I know I can hold it up so I suck it up, get on my bike and ride.

When we get to the clubhouse, Backfire backs his bike in with the other members' bikes and I put mine in the visitor area. Both areas are covered with cameras and are within the gates. I hop off and join him as he takes me by the hand and leads me inside.

I really don't think that Backfire is a hand holding type of guy most of the time, so I figure he's making a point and sure enough, as soon as we get inside, heads turn to stare at us. Some of the guys I've met snigger and smirk, while others, who are still strangers to me, look shocked.

We head to Ace as he beckons us over.

"How you doing, Kat?" he asks.

"Pretty good. Just have some aches and pains from so much walking and kicking. I'm not as fit as I could be."

"Backfire's not been giving you a workout program?" Shades smirks before he gets Backfire's fist in his gut. Not for the first time, apparently. It seems he'll never learn.

"Different muscles," I say innocently back to him. Backfire wraps an arm around me and I lean back into him, making it obvious to all that his claiming is not one sided. He gives me a quick squeeze.

"You two good?" Ace asks.

Backfire answers, "Yeah. It's official. Everyone, meet my old lady."

I can accept this term. It's just one of those expressions that have found its way into biker culture and it is what it is, just a different form of saying girlfriend and boyfriend. I even accept that there may someday be a property patch coming my way, but what I am not, nor will I ever be, is owned. I accept the protection that Backfire and his brothers are offering with the term, but that's it. Lori went over it with me at Girl's Night In, and since I've never been to a huge multi-club run or party in America before, I'm willing to give things a go. There is no point in ignoring a practice that has gone on for so long, and even recommended by the only lady biker I know here. I'll see what happens. With everything else that's happening at the moment, it's not like I want to do anything that would mess with our growing relationship. We have enough problems as it is, but hell, when a big strong man like Backfire shows you his soul, it's worth the risk to me.

"So are you ready to tell us what happened to you? Can you tell all of us?" Ace asks. I smile at him and nod.

"We'll go out to the back garage," he decides, "It's private enough there."

Whilst Ace leads the way, I follow Backfire, Trash, and Shades who are on either side of me. Way to make a girl feel protected.

The garage actually has bikes and tools in it, but also a beer fridge and a load of chairs. I personally think the sofas are overkill, but whatever makes them happy. There are prospects in sight surrounding the building, keeping others out. I sit down on a bar stool as Backfire goes to the fridge, pulling out two Diet Cokes. It didn't take him long to learn what I like. Passing me one, he leans on the wall to my side while Ace is on my other. Sugar and spice!

"For those of you who don't know, this is Kat, and Kat belongs to Backfire," Ace begins. "Kat's planning to open a business here as a custom painter and has opened up a shit storm of trouble. Trash has found out that a group of businessmen are trying to buy up all the available business land in the area and Kat put in for a unit, screwing up their plans and putting her in their sights. A bent council member was reporting Kat to the Police all the time for petty shit. That harassment came back on them when the Tinman and Kat, and I imagine Backfire, decided they want to work with each other, so I authorized that we put in for all the available units on that estate. Someone had just withdrawn from a unit big enough for Tinman; can't imagine why that was. Backfire and Shades had words with the Councilman. The bummer is that instead of all this deflecting attention from Kat, it seems to have focused it more on her and yesterday they kidnapped her. Now I'll let her tell you the story from there."

I take a deep breath and glance at Backfire. Taking a moment's strength from him, I face a room full of thirty-odd pissed off bikers.

"I didn't know there was a problem so when a councilman asked to meet me at the unit, I didn't know anything was off," I begin, "So I went along. I met him and the next thing I knew, I was grabbed from behind and rendered unconscious by some type of chemical... I imagine it was chloroform. Anyway, I came to in an empty house full of huge bugs. I wasn't tied up or anything. I think the bugs must have weakened the place because it was relatively simple to kick out the door to the room. The boards on the windows were rotten so I kicked through those too. Then I was free and simply walked away."

"How could you kick through things so easily?" a man I don't know asks in respectful tone.

"I did Tae Kwon Do for years and years," I said. "I was good at destruction against breaking boards."

"So you walked?" Sock asks.

"I walked until I started to know where I was. I didn't want to knock on people's doors in case it was the Bugmen's home. Once I knew where I was, I didn't want to go anywhere obvious like here or home, so I went to my mate Amber's and called Backfire from there. That's it, really." I'm so nervous by the end that I drink the entire can of pop that Backfire handed me earlier.

"Get yourself another one," Ace says, "Then go into the clubhouse and find the girls. Stay there while

we have a few words out here. Rusty will go with you."
I touch Backfire lightly on the leg as I leave before Ace
calls over a redheaded prospect to walk with me.

As we get to the front of the clubhouse, there is
a succession of small bangs and Rusty pushes me to
the ground, covering me with his body. I watch in
shock as the ground seems to explode with little
eruptions as the bullets hit, just like in the movies.
Thankfully they miss Rusty and me.

Gunfire?

REALLY????

What is going on?

CHAPTER 16
THE RIDE BEGINS

Backfire

The sound of gunfire galvanizes us into fuckin' action. We run off in the directions we've been allocated, to defend different areas of the clubhouse. I rush around to the front and see Rusty rolling off Kat. The bastards have targeted my girl again, and they're all gonna pay for this.

I pull her up into my arms and begin to carry her. Several other brothers cover the front so that Brewer and I can move to take Kat and Rusty to the relative safety of the back of the building where the walls of the various neighboring structures hide us from sight.

Once there, we check them for injuries. Brewer is talking to Rusty, trying to find out what happened while I just hold Kat. My girl is strong, but she's had so much happen to her in such a short space of time that it's obvious she's shaken up.

Ace comes up to me and says "Pack for a week, maybe two, then wait for me in the garage."

He turns to Kat, "What size clothes are you? I need you to have enough clothes too. I don't want you to go back to your house so is there anything there you can't live without? Medications, maybe?"

"No. I have nothing I'm desperate for at home." Then she pauses for a second to think and says, "Is it safe to go to my bike? Can you give me a minute to check it? I might not need anything."

"What do you need?" Ace asks.

"My saddlebags," she says. "I keep spare clothes there. I got into the habit with the rain in England and never thought to change it."

Ace indicates for Shades to get the bags for her. He jogs back with them.

"Thank you so much," she says as she tips the contents onto a picnic table. She pulls out two pairs of shorts, socks, a pair of jeans, chaps, vest tops and a hoodie. Add to that a couple of makeup bags, waterproofs, and a hat. What is it about women that they need all this shit with them? Kat gives me the evil eye as if guessing what I'm thinking.

"I'm nearly good," she says, "Except for knickers."

"I knew you were going to say that. There won't be any left in stock here at this rate."

"My bad," she says, not looking the least bit repentant.

Kat

Less than an hour later, four plain black Harleys, owned by the club, leaves the clubhouse. They're being ridden by Shades, Irish, Sock and Backfire, with me riding bitch. We ride north for a couple of hours until we come to a no-tell motel off the beaten track for the night.

Even though the stock bike is more comfortable for a pillion than Backfire's actual bike, with not only an easier leg position but a sissy bar, my legs still hurt, so I have a hot shower and curl up in bed to cuddle with Backfire. I'm slowly starting to get over the last few days, but I have to admit to being shaken up. In my world, kidnappings are not supposed to be real. And gunfire? What have I gotten myself into over a place to set up my shop? This is ridiculous.

I shiver and try to burrow a little deeper into Backfire's warmth. He wraps me into his arms and whispers, "Don't worry, baby. I've got you."

Even so, I had a disturbed night, waking up screaming and shaking, waking Backfire up too and having Sock and Shades burst through the connecting door into our room.

How embarrassing.

"Sorry." I say. "I suppose it's a little late to mention I get nightmares when I get really wound up?"

"Don't worry about it, babe," Sock reassures me. "I'd have nightmares if I was in bed with Backfire, too."

I buried myself in the bed and left him to 'sort out' his brothers.

Backfire

When I get back in bed, all I can do is hold my girl. I want to get her past what's happened. The plan is fuckin' simple—we ride. There was no specific destination when we left the clubhouse which cuts down on the risk of someone finding us. We'll just chill for a few days while the guys work on finding Fish and whoever else was responsible for trying to hurt Kat. I want to be part of it but right now, she's my first priority.

I have no fuckin' idea how this happened. I wasn't looking for more than a night, maybe two with anyone, but Kat? She is so fuckin' different than the women I'm used to. It's like she's from another planet, which in a way, I suppose, England is to us. I don't intend to lose her in any way, shape, or form. This shit needs to end.

CHAPTER 17

ONWARDS

Kat

I wake up in the morning totally wrapped up with Backfire.

His presence gives me the comfort I need. Once we get up, we shower and check out for the day. Over breakfast, the guys decide to ride up the East Coast for a bit. I'm cool with that idea. It sounds interesting.

We stop for lunch a couple hours down the road at a steak house—what a surprise. I sit between Backfire and Irish as I know him the least of the other guys. I realise that there are a lot of the Cycle Devils I still have yet to meet, so I ask Backfire, politely, how many members of the West Florida chapter there are and he tells me thirty-two, not including prospects.

Irish is actually Irish. He moved to America from Wexford when he was young. He was very interested when I told him that I had ridden over to bike shows in Waterford before I came here. I promised to show him the photos, but most of them are online and I'm staying off Facebook for now.

The guys order steaks, but I'm a bit worried about eating too much meat in one day. It'll send me straight to sleep. Backfire says he'll look after me, so steak it is.

We hit the coast road and I take in the scenery, and it begins to relax me. Backfire must feel something because his left hand comes off the handlebars and he reaches back to rest his hand on my thigh. How he manages to look comfortable doing this is beyond me, but I'm not complaining.

I feel myself beginning to get my head around what happened to me and to begin to mentally and physically calm down. I'm trying hard not to show it, but I'm scared, angry, nervous, vengeful, but most of all, I want time to myself so I can shut people out and deal with this on my own. I want to break down alone.

Don't think Backfire would be down with that plan, and in all honesty, locking myself away from the situation probably wouldn't help anyway.

After picking up a load of snacks and food for lunch at a petrol station, we find ourselves in one of these big US parks that you can just drive into. I love the sense of peace here. Backfire asks me if I want to stay the night. It blows my mind that you can rent lodges at a place like this. I love the trees, the beach, and the ocean. When I see the so-called lodge we have for the night, I nearly cry with relief. It's so perfect.

It's not exactly a basic lodge by any standard of the imagination. It's a three bedroom "cabin," which most definitely works for me. By the time everything is settled, it's evening, so Shades and Sock go on a beer run. The guys seem happy here too as they order in a load of pizzas and rent a movie for the night.

Sean and I call it an early night. So much has happened that I just need to catch up on myself, and my man must have understood that. He really is getting to know me

CHAPTER 18
THE STATE PARK

Kat

Backfire and I didn't exactly get up at the crack of dawn. I think this was partly due to how badly I have been sleeping recently. I must be starting to get over what has been happening. In fact, I manage to sleep through a couple of the guys going out to get breakfast and it's the smell of food that eventually wakes me up. I'm being held, warm and safe, by my man.

I turn over to see him looking at me so I smile as he pulls me to him for a good morning kiss. I never used to like kissing before I met him, especially kissing in the morning before I've brushed my teeth. Backfire doesn't exactly give me a choice in the matter and somehow that makes everything feel sexier, even things like kissing. He's not one of those awful, sloppy kissers either. His kisses are firm, confident, and sexy. All I can do is just go with the flow; learning to enjoy the things he likes. It's not hard with him at all.

"Time to get up," he says, "or the guys will start fuckin' with us. Plus, I'm hungry," he smiles. Smiling back at him, I get dressed and we go to the kitchen to see what the guys have left for us to eat.

After breakfast, we walk to the beach and settle down to enjoy the sea breeze. I absolutely love the sea. Now that I'm feeling more myself, I begin to question everything that has happened so far. When we left the clubhouse, I admit to feeling a bit shell shocked, and most definitely not at the top of my game. I didn't ask questions, I just went with what Ace said to do. Now, however, it's time to start getting a little control back in my life.

"So what exactly are we doing out here? What is the plan?" I ask.

"We're taking a short vacation. So much was going down that we felt the danger to you was too great, so we just thought it was better for you to get away while we find out exactly what's going on, so we're just chilling; staying off the radar. Everything is being looked into by the the brothers back at home. Lori told Amber you would be away with me for a few days. Trash is still looking into the units with Tinman. Some of the guys are after Fish, so in short, everything is being dealt with. We've just taken you out of the line of fire."

I look at him and resist the urge to burst into tears. "It was all just a shock, you know? Being kidnapped and shot at are not things that ever happen in my normal day. It's taking a while to sort all this out in my head, so I'm sorry that I'm being so slow about dealing with things."

He shakes his head at me and says, "No, you're not. You've been fuckin' amazing and strong about all of it. Some women, hell, even men would have collapsed in a heap and lost their shit, but not you."

I look at him and laugh, "Ladies like that are unlikely to last five minutes with you."

All the guys burst out laughing at that one.

Backfire

My girl is starting to come back to herself. I haven't known her long enough, but I do know her well enough now to be sure that she had drawn into herself because of what happened to her. More than a shock, but she's coping with it all. I'm so fuckin' proud to call her mine. I knew her legs hurt her before we left the clubhouse, but she never complained or said she'd had enough. She just carried on 'cause she's so fuckin' strong.

I watch her walking on the beach when Shade's phone rings. Ace is keeping in touch with him directly so that Kat doesn't have to worry any further.

The message from Ace shows that the boys have been making shitloads of progress. They've caught Fish. After a 'chat', they know all the details of the kidnapping, his links to the association and his involvement in the shooting.

Seems he offered to push through a land grab by the association who want to take over all the area, but he swears he doesn't know why. I suppose it doesn't really matter at this point. Fish was trying to scare Kat off in the same way he'd got rid of all the other opposition but it wasn't working. He knew the club's applications were linked to Kat so he thought kidnapping her would scare her off and he could use her to make the club back off. When it didn't work, he got desperate and tried to shoot Kat to destroy the only real evidence against him.

What a stupid fuckin' prick.

It's not the law he has to answer to, but me and my club. He fuckin' knew Kat was with us and he tried to shoot her when she was at our clubhouse. He's crazy if he thinks for a second he's gonna get a date with the law.

Kat

I go back to where Backfire and the guys are talking. Irish stands up and says, "I'm riding into town. Does anyone want anything?"

"Actually, yes," I respond, "If there's anywhere that sells it without too much effort, a sketchbook and something to draw with. If not, don't worry about it." I reach into my pocket to get my wallet out and hand him some notes.

"You have any preferences?"

"Pastels and the biggest pad you can get that won't need to fold up in the saddle bags, but honestly, whatever you can get will work."

Backfire gives me a smile. I guess he's thinking that if I'm drawing, I'm feeling better. He's not wrong.

"And a bikini too," he says to Irish. Irish skims his eyes over me, nods, and vanishes. I hide my face in my hands, knowing they all know enough about a woman's body to know my size. Still, Backfire is right. The water does appeal to me and skinny-dipping does not.

I join the guys at the table as Backfire fills me in about what the club has found out and about Fish. When he's done, I sit and mull over what he's said. I get why the guys are protecting me, and it's because I'm Backfire's girl. Some part of me wants to rail against this possessive attitude, but the other part of me revels in the feeling of security he brings.

Crazy.

Backfire

Kat has been quiet since we told her what had been happening at home, but nowhere near as fuckin' withdrawn from us as before. We're sitting together at the table by the cabin, reading a couple of biker mags online, using Socks' laptop. To be honest, we're comparing them; The British mag versus the American mag. The American mag has naked women aplenty, while the British one has women posing in clothes. The British one features far more different bike makers than the US one does. There seems to be a difference in some bike styles too, especially with baggers, bikes with fairings and hard bags that are all part of one smooth look. They don't appear to be the fashion in England.

Strangely enough, the differences between them help me understand Kat better by being able to see what kind of lifestyle she's used to.

When Irish brings her the bikini, which is fuckin' too skimpy in my opinion for my girl, she smiles wide and I follow her into the cabin to watch her change. I've pulled some boxers on for once so I can join her. I end up throwing her around in the water while she's trying to pull my boxers off. It's not a game I can return because there's no way I want my brothers seeing anymore of her than they already are. The bikini even emphasizes her tattoos—the stark, black material bringing out the bright color of the gas tanks and bikes that skim her skin. She looks amazing, and she's all mine.

Kat

After playing on the beach, we go back to the cabin, hit our room and take a shower together. We're playful as we start washing each other but that soon gives way to a lot more than play.

His kisses are soft as he starts caressing me all over. I love the way he doesn't just give a cursory grope of my boobs, thinking that's enough foreplay, but he touches me everywhere. He can play my body like it's his own personal instrument. As we start to spin out of control, he reaches for a towel and carefully dries my body before he lays me out on the bed.

I lie there quietly, watching him. The view of his perfect body is spectacular. He dries himself off while I watch him, making it into a bit of a show just for me. With a dark look in his eyes, he stares at my body, laid out bare before him, and he joins me on the bed. He maneuvers himself so that he's on top of me while his heated gaze never leaves mine. As his body looms over mine, he asks me with such seriousness, "Who do you belong to?"

Without even thinking about it, I say, "You—Only you."

"That's exactly what I need to hear, babe," and slowly he starts to rekindle the fire.

He quietly tells me all the things he is going to do to me in detail, and how he'll do it all very slowly. Fuck. That turns me on. He's going to kiss me everywhere, then lick every inch of me, ending with my pussy.

He goes on to say that after he spends time feasting between my open legs, he'll make me come twice before he replaces his tongue with his cock as he begins to fuck me senseless. It sounds like a very good plan to me.

I prepare myself for the pleasure I know without a doubt that he will give me, whilst forming my own plans to drive him crazy.

I have to be a bit more subtle in my approach, but I have plans to make him beg me for more.

If I can get in a good old-fashioned sixty-nine, that would surely do the job. Mind you, it might be hard to concentrate with so much going on at the same time, so much over-stimulation, but maybe if I just drop to my knees in front of him before he gets a chance to start, that'll do the trick? What man turns down a blowjob? Certainly not mine, so I put my very subtle plan into action and by the hair pulling and moans of pleasure, he really seems to appreciate my efforts.

CHAPTER 19
I'M SO EXCITED...

Kat

The following morning, Backfire is awake way before me. He has a cup of coffee in his hands as he comes to see me before I go down to breakfast. "Ace called. He wants us to stay here for at least another couple of days."

As I try to steal a sip of his coffee I reply, "What a disaster. I hope you told him how hard that'll be."

"Get up," he says, slapping me on my bum. "Get your own coffee, too."

"What's going on, Backfire? Have I got more to worry about?"

"Babe, I think you get that I'm your man and you're my woman," he starts. "Part of being my woman means the club will take care of you, so you don't have to worry. They're dealing with this shit."

I sort of knew this, but it's difficult getting my head around it, but I've decided to be more accepting of it. Things had gotten way more scary than this girl can cope with on her own, so maybe it's just as well. Before we left, one of the club girls had acted scornful toward me over the attention I was getting for being kidnapped and shot at. For her sake, it was a good thing that none of the guys had seen what went down, but Lori had and nearly ripped her to shreds. I was on a tight time schedule but I remember her ripping into the slut about not slagging someone off until you'd been through the same thing yourself.

I grinned to myself about it as I got dressed. I just finished getting ready when Backfire came back, and this time with a box and a cup of coffee for me.

"You're not properly dressed," he said. I look at him a bit taken aback.

"Hey, I've even got knickers and a bra on. How am I not dressed?"

"You forgot this," he says, throwing a leather waistcoat at me.

I pick it up and turn it so that I can see the patches on the outside. BACKFIRE'S PROPERTY PATCH. It's one thing in theory to decide that I want to give it a go, but you still could have knocked me down with a feather when he produced it. Apparently, Shades had carried it in his saddlebags for Backfire so I wouldn't know he had it until he wanted me to. Theory and reality sometimes feel different, but I bite the bullet and go for it. I put the leather gilet on. He knows me well enough to have got me a style of leather that I really like and feel comfortable in, and I do like things that cover my bum. I suspect that Lori might have had something to do with his choice from the day we went shopping, but I'm not going to question his gesture. There is fire in his eyes as he watches me do a twirl in his colours.

Even before I finish checking myself out in the mirror, he's on me, grabbing at me and throwing me onto the bed. He strips me and then tells me to put the rag back on. This time there is no gentle; it is total possession and dominance. He must really like what he sees because he takes me from behind on all fours, spreading me wide—really going deep. I love it. This man can give it to me any way he wants, whenever he wants.

Backfire

Seeing my woman wearing nothing but my property rag is the absolute fuckin' best. She's sexy as fuck. In fact, I can't think of anything sexier. I want her so badly at this moment I can't hold back. When I eventually slow down, it becomes clear that I don't fuckin' need to. My woman is with me and riding my cock like she owns it, which she sure as fuck does.

After we fuck, we have a quick shower before I take my properly dressed woman out to show her off to my brothers. I never expected to feel this way about any woman. Nearest thing I can describe it to is pride, but it's not that. I mean, I'm proud that this woman is mine, but this feels like so much more than that.

My brothers don't let me down. They gather around us, giving me man hugs while Kat gets actual hugs. At this moment, I don't even fuckin' mind. We're celebrating after all, but they'd better not get into the habit of thinking they can touch her whenever they want.

After the hug fest, Kat asks, "What are we doing today?"

"Today we're going to start on your 'Living in America' educational program. Your first lesson will be learning to shoot."

She digests this, grins and says, "Ok. Where?"

Irish replies, "There's a local chapter of Cycle Devils here. Now that the worst of the threat against you is over, we can go and meet them."

"Do I need to wear anything special?" she asks.

"Nervous?" Sock teases her, pissing me off.

"A little," she replies, "I get to meet another chapter of the Devils and I still don't feel I know an awful lot. I still don't even know everyone in your chapter. I'm not sure of all the rules and such. Plus, shooting is something I never really thought about until Backfire mentioned it. I just need to get my head around the idea, so by the time we get there, I'm sure I'll be fine."

"You'll be fine, Kat." I tell her, "Just stay close and if you're nervous, keep quiet. That way, nothing can go wrong while you're finding your feet. And if anyone dares to question you, they'll have me to answer to!"

CHAPTER 20
CHARLESTON CYCLE DEVILS

Kat

We arrive at the Charleston CDMC clubhouse, which isn't actually in Charleston, but just outside the city by a minor highway. It looks like an old bar or roadhouse with an old motel behind the main building that looks like it fell into decline when the new highway came through. Now it's a fenced off compound like I always imagined US biker clubhouses to look. Beyond the buildings, it looks like it leads into a forest, and there doesn't appear to be any neighboring buildings nearby. Good thing for them, I suppose. I worked out that this is why Backfire wanted me to have his property patch away from his clubhouse. I can already see the benefits.

I stand behind him as I'm not really sure of the correct protocol, but this seems like the way to go. None of the guys address me, and Backfire doesn't introduce me. I start to get a little pissed when he's talking and Shades slyly squeezes my hand in warning while Irish gives me a slight shake of his head. Fine. I'll just keep a lid on it for a little while longer and see what happens next.

The guys proceed to the bar. Shades is buying so he raises an eyebrow at me, "Diet?" he asks. I smile and give him a nod.

Backfire sits on a barstool and pulls me to stand between his legs, "Thanks for keeping quiet, Kat. It helps us not to draw any more attention to you than being my property fuckin' will."

I quietly work through that comment and my anger starts to chill. The others look at us, knowing I'm still getting my head around things.

"So aren't you going to ask anything?" Backfire pushes.

"Actually I wasn't, but if you want to tell me when we're doing this gun thing, I'm all ears," I smile at him and the guys laugh.

"After we've had our drink," and then he laughs as I turn in his arms to hug him.

Backfire

It fuckin' kicks ass to see my girl excited. As we walk closer to the gun range, I can literally feel the excitement coming off her. I did have plans to go through gun parts and cleaning and putting a gun together, but I realize now isn't the time. The new plan is to let her just shoot. I have a little collection of different guns for her to try that the local brothers have lent us. I hope they'll have a gun that she likes and fits her well.

I tell her the revised plan as we get to the range. My brothers help me and soon there is a line-up of different shapes, grips, and calibers of handguns sitting on the table. My brothers and I have decided to try a few different guns ourselves. It's rare for me to let someone else touch my gun, but you never know. There might be a gun here I might like to own.

We explain the basic rules for today to Kat. She'll fire on her own. A gun will be handed to her and she is only allowed to point it at the target or the ground—no walking around or anything like that to start with; just point, aim and fire. When it's our turn, she is to stand behind us, away from the gun table. I know it's fuckin' baby steps, but who wants a fuckin' accident here, especially from a total newbie, no matter how responsible she might be otherwise.

So it begins.

My brothers shoot first to show Kat the right way to set yourself up and to get her used to the noise before it's her turn. We're not great on protective equipment here. As she's already been shot at, she pretty much understands that they'll be no use to her if she's attacked again so she doesn't raise an eyebrow at this. Gotta love my girl's strength.

It starts out slow, but before I know it, she has a shit-eatin' grin on her face and already has the hang of it. I fuckin' love seeing such a carefree smile on that beautiful face of hers.

Eventually when she's tried all the different guns, she asks to try a particular one again. I thought she would have done so sooner but I have to respect her for trying all the options available to her. She chooses a lightweight .38 designed for ladies. Repeatedly, she uses the same gun and her improvement with it is unbelievable. I reckon we'll have to sort out some licenses, knowing my girl, and get her one. The best part is that it's red, not pink like some of the guns here. It's a chick thing. I am not fuckin' buying anyone a pink gun, not even Kat.

Kat

I have to say that I'm impressed with how the guys have arranged this. It feels right. I know it's set up as a taster session, but when we get back, I'll look up gun safety and stuff like that.

I like this gun. Most of the other .38's I tried were bigger and heavier, but this is small and designed for a woman's hand, therefore the grip is also smaller. It's definitely the most comfortable gun to use here, even better than the smaller calibers that I tried, so I spend the rest of the time practicing until the guys are done. I make a mental note of what sort of gun it is that I like because I foresee one coming my way in the future.

After all, a girl's gotta shop.

They go to the table and make the guns safe, doing the manly backslapping thing, looking like they've conquered the world.

Men!

They're just so easy to please.

CHAPTER 21

AGAIN?

Kat

I'm feeling pretty psyched as we walk back to the clubhouse. The guys can tell and so they start in on teasing me. They're not going to ruin my good mood.

I'm one of those people who just love to learn new skills. Whether I'll ever consider using a gun for anything other than target practice is a whole different ballgame, but still, I suppose it might have some use as a deterrent. There are also significantly different wild animals here than in England, and whilst it's not my intention to go hunting or deliberately hurt something, you never know when you could use it. I've been on some horse riding holidays in the West, in Wyoming and Montana, when I was younger and a responsible adult always took a rifle in case of emergencies. Bears and such apparently can be dangerous, but luckily we never saw one.

To say we aren't exactly concentrating is no understatement, but to come around the corner into a gang of masked men with guns?

Oh God. Not again!

CHAPTER 22
HOW FUCKING DARE THEY!

Backfire

I've got to stay with my girl. I can see her start to turn in on herself again and my brothers see it too, so they take the lead as I pull Kat closer to me.

"No, Mr. Backfire. We'll be taking the young lady with us," one of them says.

I feel Kat start to shake. One of them reaches forward to grab Kat and there isn't a whole lot I can do to stop him as all of us are individually covered by guns to the head. Kat though, she grabs him and manages to pull his mask off. I instantly recognize him as a hang around from the Charleston clubhouse.

"That was unfortunate, but you might as well know this," the man speaks, "We have people in all your little clubhouses. You're no match for my employers."

Sock pipes up, "You sure you don't want to tell us more?"

"You sure think you're clever, don't ya," he replies, "Why no, Mr. Sock. I don't believe I do."

But in a way he does tell us something more. He tells us that the association's minions know us all by name. Not a great development.

"We'll be taking Miss Kat with us, so I think it will be best if you all are immobilized before we leave."

Some of the bastards produce zip ties and soon they have us all tied up, hands behind our backs and our ankles fastened tight. I am fuckin' beyond furious. I'm going to kill every fuckin' one of them.

"I suggest, Miss Kat, that you come with us. Don't cause any further unpleasantness because I would hate to destroy everything you love, starting with these disreputable characters."

How the hell did these hillbilly dipshits, who think they speak so fuckin' proper, get into our club? How was this missed, and how many have infiltrated our clubhouses?

I watch as Kat looks at him with blank eyes, but with her hand behind her back, she waves at me. Looks like my clever girl is not as beaten as she appears.

Kat

I DON'T FUCKING BELIEVE THIS.

I've been shot at and kidnapped not once, but twice. Enough is enough. I am no longer scared or feeling frozen; I am pissed off. With the guys tied up and so many men against me, I have to play it smart, so I pretend to be terrified. Since these people have had balls enough to shoot at me before, it's not really hard. I can play dumb. I attempt to appear to go along with what he says, but I'm waiting for my moment.

The thugs start to lead me away from the guys. I look back to see the fury and understanding in

Backfire's eyes. At least he gets the message that I haven't given in.

CHAPTER 23

GAMES IN THE WOODS

Kat

We don't travel far before I have a little "accident." I go over on my ankle and pretend that I've hurt it far worse than it actually is. Although they appear frustrated, no one tries to carry me so they have to slow down to my injured pace. I will play this for all I can 'til Backfire and the boys can get to me.

Backfire

As soon as those stupid fucks are out of sight, some of my brothers from the Charleston club appear from the bushes and free us. They're led by their Vice-President, Mad Mick. The name pretty much says it all.

Mick waits until we're all on our feet and starts to lead us in a different direction than the one Kat was taken in. I start to object but he tells me, in no uncertain term, to get my shit together and trust them to know what is going on here.

That shit's easier said than done. They have my old lady.

We soon join a large group of brothers from three different chapters; West Florida, Myrtle Beach, and Charleston. Mick explains that they couldn't draw attention to the fact that they knew what was happening by all leaving the clubhouse at once, so they called in outside help. Makes sense, and it's good to have people from my chapter here.

We slowly start to make our way around to the site where the kidnappers' van is parked. Luckily, they don't know their way around the grounds as well as we do, so it's easy for us to get around quickly. Once we arrive at their van, we find that Tinman has been having fun with their engine.

Kat

The slow progress we make is not only due to my ankle, but these thugs are trying to make sure that no one is following them. They are so worried about it that they are taking even more time getting to their destination. This is a mistake on their part, in my opinion. This is only giving Backfire more time to help me, and of course, I see no reason to point this out to them. I want to see the surprise on their faces when they realise how stupid this idea of theirs was.

Backfire

Now that we're in the clearing, we split back into our own chapters. Ace looks grim as he tells us that Brewer is working on finding out who the traitor is in our club. I've never seen him so fuckin' angry, so I'm pretty sure whoever it is is not going to enjoy the fuckin' rest of his very short life.

I find out there are forty odd Cycle Devils here, meaning the future is not looking too fuckin' bright for the men who took Kat.

Snack, the Charleston President, comes over and tells me to go with the ambush squad. The sooner Kat's with me, the better. He and Ace think it's a good idea to send some of my chapter brothers as a group with me to get Kat to safety. I want to kill, but I want to get Kat even more. Trash, Shades, Bullet and Tinman are to be my backup.

We go into the woods to find the ambush point and wait. I can't fuckin' believe these kidnappers are so slow, but I'll take it. They'll fall right into our hands.

Kat

One minute I'm being escorted by my kidnappers and the next, about twenty Cycle Devils appear out of the woods. In a fleeting glance, I don't recognise any of them, but in the space of time that that glance took, two Cycle Devils are escorting me into the woods, whilst the last glance I see of what's happening is that every thug kidnapper has one of the Cycle Devils' guns pointed individually at them.

I'm escorted a little way into the woods when I see Backfire and other guys I know. The relief is incredible. The whole process couldn't have taken longer than an hour from start to finish, but even so, I'm alive and back with my man.

Backfire

Kat's whisked away before the kidnappers can react. Our attack team is that fuckin' fast. I guess that's what happens when you have guys who have been in various branches of the military. There's a whole mixture of different arms of the service represented in our club. From what I know, most MCs are the same. The best part is that Kat doesn't see what happens to the kidnappers; she has enough on her mind without the images of violence my brothers rain down on them, and certainly doesn't need to fuckin' know or see the torture that will occur before they die.

My brothers give Kat to me and go back to the kidnappers. I wrap myself around her as she clings to me for dear life while I hold onto her just as fiercely. I keep coming too close to losing her and this has to fuckin' stop. With Kat in my arms, I just want to hold her here forever. When did I become so fuckin' soft? After a few moments, I come back to what's going on around me, only to hear the kidnappers being herded into a clearing by the rest of my brothers.

Kat

"Backfire, it's always been a fantasy of mine to be rescued by a tall, dark, handsome man." I say as I snuggle into him as he bursts out laughing along with the others.

"My ankle hurts. I went over on it to slow them down and pretended it was worse than it really was, but can we walk back slowly guys?" Well that changed the atmosphere quickly. Note to self; don't tell these guys you're hurt. It brings out their protective nature.

"Let's have a look then," Bullet says. I don't know him very well, but Backfire makes no comment so it must be alright. I take my boot off to survey the damage as Bullet pulls a first aid kit out of his backpack, "I used to be an army medic."

I grimace as Bullet straps my ankle up. Maybe this wasn't the cleverest plan, but it did help give the Cycle Devils time to get into position.

"How did you know that this would happen? How did any of you know to be ready for it?"

Bullet grins and says, "The hang-around that was in place at Myrtle Beach flipped and decided that he liked the club better than working with those association assholes, so Spook, the Myrtle Beach Prez, cut him a deal."

I didn't realise the full extent of what I was taking on when I agreed to take on Backfire's club. It's pretty incredible, and something I really need time to take in.

CHAPTER 24
AFTERMATH

Backfire

As we get back to the clubhouse, I place Kat with her legs up on the leather sofa by the bar. I can tell she's thinking about putting them down until she decides that it's comfortable like this and goes with it. One of the bartenders acts like a waitress and brings her over a Diet Coke and some beer for the men. On the tray is a huge bar of English chocolate, which Kat pounces on. Soon she's guzzling her drink and scoffing down her chocolate. I decide to just chalk it up to the fuckin' madness that is my woman.

Kat

My day has significantly improved. Chocolate does that to a girl. When Ace and the other Presidents come over, everyone except for Backfire leaves.

Ace introduces Spook and Snack as they pull up seats around us. I go to put my leg down to give them more room when Backfire grabs my legs and keeps them where they are.

After they do a double check and see that I'm fine, they ask if I would answer some questions. Before I can speak, Backfire agrees for me.

Ace starts the questioning by wanting a virtual word for word repeat of everything the men said. I have to disappoint them by saying the only things they said to me when I was alone with them were things like, "come on" and "hurry up."

Ace brushes this away, but he's clearly disappointed that there's no more information to be given.

I'm beyond shocked that all these guys have put themselves in danger for me, well, for Backfire. I still think our relationship is new and there are still loads of things we need to learn about each other, but at the moment, nothing matters to them apart from Backfire's claim on me.

I risk a look at Backfire first then ask, "So what happens next?"

"Next is that you get better and maybe try to stay out of trouble for a little while," Ace says. "Start making plans for your business and seeing if you can work with Backfire and Tinman. We're struggling to keep up with your adventures."

"I'll try," I promise. That must have been the right thing to say because I get a squeeze from Backfire and smiles from all the men.

Go me.

Backfire

Kat's in bed, fast asleep. Now, it's time for me to play. My brothers have been questioning the kidnappers all day, and everything they know so far has been acquired by various methods. Shades and I join them, and I watch Trash with a boyish grin on his face and blood on his hands. If the women who chase him think he's not as tough as the rest of us and is only a member to be a club lawyer, they're so fuckin' wrong. If they could fuckin' see him now.

"Hi. I got all the info they had. Ace and the other Prez have been putting together a plan, so all that we needed was some vermin extermination. That one's weak; blood loss from losing a few body parts."

I smile slowly. I get to finish these fuckin' scums off, and I will, but I shoot them so they'll bleed out. Wouldn't want it quick now, would we? I stand and watch until they all die, then I start to dispose of the bodies. AJ from Charleston comes over and says, "Go back to your girl in case she wakes up. She'll probably be happier if you're there."

"Thanks, man. I owe you."

CHAPTER 25|
ONE MONTH LATER
PLAN MAKING

Kat

I love my man!

I think he loves me.

Things with Backfire are going really well. We are having fun together doing normal things that don't involve kidnapping or being shot at. Amongst other things we've been going shooting together regularly and I'm getting quite good. It's much better being on the pointy end of the gun and not the receiving end.

We ride together, we hang out together, we go to the clubhouse together, and we party together. I now know all the members of the chapter by name and their old ladies, and even their kids. One big, happy family.

We go to lots of bike nights all over Florida. My excuse being I want to look at the different styles of custom paintwork that are popular here. It's a hard way to do research, but someone has to do it.

Wednesday night is still girls' night with Amber and Lori, we are often joined by Wizz, who I really get on well with. She does leather and loads of other things.

On some other nights the guys are away I invite more of the club sisters around and they all accept Amber too. We are all just a bunch of women having a laugh. The offer does not extend to the sluts who hang round the club as I can't seem to find much common ground with them. Bizarre.

I don't have nightmares anymore, but I don't like being left on my own too much. I imagine this feeling will fade with time. I'm a work in progress, but there you go.

Backfire

We've a lot of business on the table at Church this Wednesday. After the routine officers' reports we get down to the shit that's been happenin'

Brewer leans forward and reports, "While you guys were rescuing Kat I found our mole and held him in our warehouse, where Trash and I had a few words with him before he had a little accident. There is no further infiltration of our club and the chapter sergeants have all rooted out the shit from their own clubhouses, so the MC is clean." We bang the table in approval.

Trash presents the situation with the units. "The association seem to have withdrawn their opposition to the purchase of units by the club and Kat, thinking we wouldn't have the money for everything we put in for, which is pretty much a fortune, but they'd be wrong. The process will be finalized in the next few days so we need to make final plans for getting the units up and running."

Ace sums up. "We can fill all the space we've got. Backfire and Tinman have their custom shop with Kat's paintworks. CC and Bullet's old ladies, Jewels and Wizz, have a business working with leather, and Cobra and Tex's screenprint machine can fit in with them. We good?"

Nods all round the table. Irish speaks up. "Have we got too much to defend in one place here? Three old ladies at least as well as the machines and equipment all stuck out in the open?"

Bullet's right on this. "We can cover one entrance and exit a lot easier than units stuck all over the city as we have now. The businesses complement each other so they'll trade off each other too. We've four brothers based on site permanently anyway as well as the ladies."

OB asks if anyone needs to call on club resources to set up beyond the acquisition of the units. Everyone's good.

Then Ace moves on to next business. "I need a package to go up to Jake, the Louisville president. Backfire, you want to handle this, maybe see your folks?"

"Always, brother, is it acceptable to take Kat with me?"

"It will be. The package is nothing dangerous and we've no problems along the road." With that the gavel goes down and we pile into the bar.

Ace wanders over to me "How are things with you and Kat?"

"Fuckin' great. Thanks for the opportunity to run up to Louisville. I get to take Kat away and meet my folks, and have a break from the crazy shit that is the business. She's got lists made to organise her other lists, whatever the fuck that's about. It also gives us some time alone, just the two of us, on a decent-length ride to see how we cope with no distractions."

"It's all good. Ride safe, brother"

CHAPTER 26
KENTUCKY

Backfire

The run up to Kentucky is a good ride, nice and long, but not too long. Instead of sleeping on the ground we stay at motels, not the fuckin' grandest places in the Universe but better than camping, not that I think Kat would complain, just that I want to look after my girl.

It feels good to ride with her by my side as we eat up the miles. We ride together, eat together, shower together, and do everything else imaginable together. It's just the two of us and it's all good. We have a smooth ride with no trouble and we're both in a good mood when we reach Louisville. We go to the clubhouse first, 'cause business (and fuckin' definitely club business) before pleasure. Mom and my old man meet us there.

I can tell Kat's nervous, but I hold her in reassurance.

I hug Pop as Mom holds back, waiting her turn. Then he comes for Kat as I greet Mom.

"Liam," he says, holding out his arm.

"Hound of Ulster," she replies, taking in his road name, CuChulainn off his colours. "I'm Katrina, but most people call me Kat."

"You know the stories," he says with a grin.

"Oh yes, I grew up on them. My granddad was Irish."

"Well, this is my wife, Mary," he says.

"Hello, Kat. It's great to finally meet you," she says with a smile.

I go into the office to pay my respects to Jake, the President and deliver Ace's package. Then we move to the bar where loads of the brothers greet me. The prospect behind it looks too long and too closely at Kat, even though she's wearing my property patch. It's not only me, but the Louisville brothers catch him too. Their Sergeant at Arms, Bats, named for his favorite toys (any game will do, I've even heard he has a cricket bat in his collection) pulls him outside for a little discussion. I don't think he'll be doing that again. Another prospect quickly comes over and begins getting our drinks to us. Kat doesn't even bat a lash. She's learning, too. After that the night proceeds with everyone making us welcome.

Kat

I ignored the incident at the clubhouse and let it go because it's not my business and nothing I can do can change it. I continue the night hanging with Mary and her friends, then we go to Liam and Mary's ranch. Even in the dark I can see it's a beautiful property. Mary offers us supper but we're tired so we just go to bed.

"Well, this is awkward," Mary says at breakfast after a couple of minutes of silence. "What's the matter with you all?"

"You're going to be my mother in law, have you heard all the scary stories about them?" I venture. "I might be feeding your son the wrong food or something."

Mary throws her head back and laughs, "Well, if he eats it, it's right. He can stand up for himself," she grins. "I'm more interested in getting to know you, apart from bikes, books, art, and crafting, is there anything else you like? Anything you did in England you don't do here?"

"Ride horses. I want everything to get stable here before I get a horse, if you'll pardon the pun. I've found some stables pretty close——I even went for a ride out there when I first came here. I was absolutely amazed at all the horses in the area."

"I didn't know that," Backfire says to me, "I ride too and Mom has horses."

"Well now that the ice is cracked," Liam says, "let's talk horses."

After breakfast, we do more than talk horses. We saddle up and Liam and Mary take us around the farm on horseback. I admit that I haven't ridden properly in Western style much, so Backfire takes great pleasure in being my instructor. I think he gets a kick out of being allowed to tell me what to do.

The ranch is beautiful and I soon start to relax with the new tack. We get back and take some time to check out the house and barns. It becomes easy to work out whose bits are whose. It's a fabulous setup and I love it. A couple of the hounds are clearly happy to have Backfire about and stick to him like glue.

Once I've been shown everything, we all sit around an outside table and have a drink. I drink a Diet Coke whilst everyone else has coffee while we start to plan our stay. Mary says she'll do some more Western riding with me, but before we do, we decide to go and do some shopping for the essentials; cider and a riding kit. Why are Sean and Liam rolling their eyes? Bizarre.

CHAPTER 27

SIX WEEKS LATER

FAMILY RIDE

Kat

I wake up in Backfire's bed at the clubhouse on the Saturday morning of the family run with a bounce.

"Babe, it's too early to get up," he grumbles.

"I want to help with breakfast," I explain as I start to get dressed.

"Wake me up when it's ready," he says as he rolls over.

Oh well. I can't be bothered with Mr. Grump this morning because the club is going out on a family ride today and I can't wait.

I hit the kitchen to find it's already starting to buzz. A round of "Morning, Kat," greets me as I make my way through.

"Hey Kat," Lori says. "Would you mind setting the table?"

"No problem." I start to gather the things I need, beginning with stuff to clean the tables. I'm just setting the tables when the guys start to arrive.

"Morning. Those tables are wiped off guys. Give me two seconds and I'll get you some plates and find out when breakfast will be ready."

"Thanks," Bullet says. No matter how much I know I owe this man and how much he's done for me, I'm still a bit wary of him and treat him with the utmost respect.

Pagan brings them out a pot of coffee and I grab some mugs. When the guys are all seated, we go into overdrive to get things ready. Sock has been bringing around a girl named Christine, who is with us this morning. She has no problems with jumping in and helping out, and we all thank her.

"I'm just going to give Backfire a shout," I say.

Lori looks around and grins, "Everyone's up early. At this rate, we'll be ready to roll at least an hour earlier than we'd originally planned. I love when men learn to follow a plan."

Backfire

We all load up on the bikes. We really need to do more of these family rides, but it's always about timing. We have four chapters in Florida and we don't have any hassle with any of the other clubs in the state at the moment, so we can pretty much go anywhere within reason.

We're meeting near the Everglades today. The Florida chapters clubbed together and bought some land with a big old fuckin' hotel on it so we can meet up and party overnight. Kat and I loaded our bikes up yesterday with everything we'd need, along with some food for the run. We're creating a fifth chapter, Everglades, out of the retired members who look after the site for us. We have enough room for everyone to have a bedroom, but the prospects have to fuckin' share.

When Tex is happy everything is ready to go, he signals to Ace who starts his bike. At his signal, other bikes start up and we set out in club order. Lori, Kat, and Sock's new girl ride their bikes at the very back, behind our pick up van, but everyone is keeping an eye on them.

We only ride for a couple of hours before pulling into a truck stop. Tex has added a couple of pit stops for the ladies and sure enough, they're all heading that way.

Do women have small bladders?

I have more fuckin' sense than to ask.

We arrive and settle in to our room. Kat's gone to sort food with the women when there's a knock on the door. I open it to find my blood brothers outside.

"Hey, I wasn't expecting you two."

"We came down to escort Jean. He's meeting the local presidents so we've got some spare time to hunt you out and meet your lady. We'll stay over at your clubhouse on the way back to New Orleans."

Day just got even fuckin' better.

"So fuckin' pleased you'll meet Kat."

"Are you serious about her?"

"Yes. I've even taken her up to the ranch to meet the folks."

"We heard. That made their year. Mom's got you married off already."

"It's a possibility, brothers."

Kat

We meet the other chapters and I watch as the guys give back thumps all around. There are things to do throughout the day. Everyone pitches in to sort the food out and many hands make light work. The men set up a bike rodeo outside with all kinds of games.

There is a covered area outside where some of the women set up and push tables together so we can all be together in a group. Others bring buckets of ice filled with beer and pop out.

I settle down where I can see what the men are doing. As they start playing games, I go over with Pagan and Christine to watch. "This is the slow race," Pagan says. "The winner is the one who finishes last." We watch it for a bit and then move along.

We come across a more rowdy group in an area lined with straw bales, on which men seemed to be falling regularly, which I'm sure isn't the game. They're riding what appear to be barstools converted into quads around a little course. We join in the general laughter at the guys' antics.

Christine says "I've seen this in a video from an online magazine. The guys there fell off a lot too," which causes us all to giggle.

"You sound happy," Backfire says from behind me.

I turn and grin at him, "That looks fun," I say and point to the flying bar stools.

Shades and Trash move over to look. Trash is dragging Pagan and Christine with him by putting his arms around their waists. That soon brings Sock and Rusty. Sean has two other blokes from the New Orleans chapter with him.

"Kat, these are my brothers; Seamus, also known as Vike and Ultan, known as Templar."

"Wow. Irish and historical names. It's wonderful to meet you." I say as I reach out to hug them. Then I look at Backfire, "You never said we'd be meeting them here, and why haven't you got a sexy historical name too? Like Saxon or something?"

"Didn't know they'd be here, babe. They just came in with their President, but they're staying over with him at our clubhouse for a few days."

I positively beam at this. "That's wonderful."

"As for his name, he's he never eaten baked beans around you?" Ultan pipes up. Unlike Shades, Ultan knows when to duck.

"Don't listen to him, babe. I got my name because my plans never backfire," he says.

"Don't you mean the other way around?" Seamus questions, but he's just not quick enough to dodge Backfire's blow to the gut.

"Are you going to put my woman down?" Backfire grumps.

"She's our sister and she started it," replies Ultan.

Backfire just shakes his head and pulls me to him as we walk over to the others. Pagan says, "I want to see the barrel racing," so we move around to another sandy area where three barrels have been set up. "In a horse rodeo, this would be an event for women, but here the guys do it on bikes," Pagan informs us.

"I've seen that in Wyoming when I was on holiday there years ago," I reply. "This seems pretty exciting too."

Rusty says there'll be a couple of games later on. "There's potato in a Haystack, where the women ride bitch and dive into a haystack when the music stops and the first one out with a potato wins."

"What else?" I ask.

"Bite the wienie, which is where a hot dog sausage is hung up and the woman riding bitch bites off as much as she can. Whoever gets the most wins."

"I wouldn't mind having a go at the potato thing," I say.

"Maybe we could all play," Pagan says.

The guys nod and walk over to see if we can register. I don't win, but it was fun and also took up a great deal of the afternoon.

We continue to party into the night. Backfire never leaves my side, so we spend the majority of the night with Seamus, Ultan, Trash, Shades, Sock and Christine. Everyone seems to be enjoying themselves; eating, drinking, and people watching, or at least I am. Christine is too, and we start to compare notes. Ultan catches us and calls us out. He's definitely the one with the sense of humour.

"We were just looking and learning," I say, going for innocence.

"Yeah, right," he says, completely unconvinced.

In the morning, after breakfast, we all help tidy up and then head back. We're joined by Ultan and Seamus, along with their President, Jean, after Jean Lafitte; the infamous privateer. They stay for another day before they head home, and Sean and I spend as much time as we can with them. It's really great that I really like his brothers and they like me, Sean is well pleased about this too.

Backfire

Ace calls a club meeting on Monday night. Jean, Ultan, and Seamus are present; my brothers flanking their president. Ace hands the meeting over to Jean.

"So, let's just dive in. The businessmen who were giving you shit may have pulled back, but they haven't left the fight altogether. They've made a deal with the Nightmare Dead MC to support them while the Dead take us on. The Dead are recruiting at the moment. They don't appear to be ready to go against us, but they're making moves. Not only have they increased the number of prospects they're taking on, but they've got whole clubs prospecting for them. They still seem to have an issue with Backfire's lady, so that's why you guys are getting a personal heads up. I'll hand you back to Ace."

Ace looks grimmer than usual, "The Florida presidents have met and we think that it's a good move to get that fifth chapter going. A lot of our members are older 'cause they've retired here. We need to start actively recruiting younger men. If you've got any proposals, come see the Officers after the meeting. With the hotel, we can house a load of brothers should the need arise, and the presidents of the chapters have agreed to send two or three brothers from each chapter as a central reserve. We can only assume they've got partial intel on us 'cause they picked up an ex-prospect from Louisville."

"Shit," I say, "that'll be the fucker they ran off for eyeing Kat."

"Poor Kat. All this trouble seems to involve her," says Trash, "Best she doesn't find out about this."

"I don't spill club business, brother," I snarl

"This isn't the time for this shit," Ace says, "Just everyone make sure they keep half an eye on her. Meeting's over."

CHAPTER 28
TWO MONTHS LATER
REAL PROGRESS

Backfire

All the businesses are up and running and everyone is doing great.

We're making a bike I designed to enter into a custom show at local bike night level. I designed it, Tinman fabricated it, Kat painted it, and the ladies did the leather seat. Cobra and Tex have printed t-shirts as part of the publicity for the bike. It's amazing, and our chances are pretty good. If we win, it should give us all another push forward.

On a different note, we've not heard shit concerning the Nightmare Dead, but every chapter's computer guy is monitoring everything about them and comparing notes weekly. We're not going to be caught off guard. We have, I have, too much at stake.

Kat

Life is good. Backfire has officially moved into my house, well, our house, but he still keeps his room at the club so we can party and not worry about getting home. I think I worry more than him. I've been brainwashed I suppose. Drunk driving is BAD.

Everything is going crazy good.

Backfire and I are going out for dinner tonight to our favourite restaurant. I don't know what the occasion is, but he has said to dress up, and that sounds good to me. I haven't had an excuse to dress up in a long time. I'm looking forward to it.

Backfire

I can't fuckin' believe this. How fuckin' stressed am I?

No one knows that I plan to ask Kat to marry me tonight. No one even suspects, so I could wimp out and not ask her.

She looks beautiful tonight in her little green dress that fits tight to her ass and then gets wider at the bottom, just above her knees with a pair of knee-high boots. She is so fuckin' hot, and she's mine.

Ask her, or just tell her?

Fuck.

Kat

We get to the restaurant and Backfire starts acting strange. Thinking about it, he's been a bit weird for the last couple of days, but I put it down to all the competitions we have lined up, but now I'm not so sure.

It's not so much anything he says or does that's weird, it's how he does it. We're sitting at the table, waiting for our food whilst I debate with myself about asking him straight out what the problem is when it all becomes clear.

"We're getting married," he states, "Give me your hand."

I shakily lift my left hand to him, too stunned to disobey. He produces a ring box out of his pocket and slips a ring onto my ring finger.

OH. MY. GOD.

I sit still, absolutely STUNNED.

I look at Backfire again as he breathes a sigh of relief.

I hand him my napkin to help wipe the sweat from his face.

I guess we are engaged.

Backfire

After we eat, we head out to the clubhouse. We go to the bar and before I even have time to make the announcement, the damn prospect behind the bar shouts out, "They're engaged!" He'll never get my vote now, big-mouthed fucker.

After the whoops and catcalls start to die away, it doesn't take long for the so-called comedians that are my brothers, to start in on me. Luckily, Kat is surrounded by old ladies examining the ring, all starting to make plans before these clowns start in on her too. If one of them upset her today, there will be hell to pay, but since she's happy, I'll suffer these fools gladly. Well, apart from Shades, whose stomach strangely hits my fist. How fuckin' clumsy of him.

CHAPTER 29
LEATHER AND STEEL

Kat

Even when I was a little girl, I dreamt of a biker wedding; none of this fairytale princess stuff for me. As I got older, I fancied the idea of getting married in white leather – white leather jeans, boots, and jacket – so I've passed this information on to my girls Amber, Lori, Pagan, Wizz and Jewels.

Wizz and Jewels are making the leathers for me and my wedding party. There are six of them, including Jack, when she gets here. I think that's a lot, but apparently that's really small for a wedding here.

I'll be riding a white Harley too. A spare bike never hurt anyone, and after the wedding I can change the paint. so all I have to do is think about underwear and a top, along with some jewellery. Oh, and buy the boots. I call Lori and Amber and see if they're for up for a bit of a shopping trip. It would really surprise me if they weren't.

Backfire and I are getting married at the clubhouse. It's being smartened up, *again*, for the ceremony. There was even a suggestion that Trash be the celebrant, but that just didn't seem right, so Preacher, one of the brothers from Miami, is going to do it for us.

My family are coming too. Who knows what family dramas a wedding will bring.

"We could go to Vegas and do the deed, then no one can interfere. We just have the reception here for them, you know, give them a party," I suggest to Backfire. "If we're already married, the whole objection thing is pretty moot."

"Not a bad idea, but what about the brothers?"

"Yeah, I don't suppose everyone could just fly to Vegas. Shame though, I don't know what it is about weddings that always seem to cause family drama. We could ask anyone who wants to go. We could have a bike parade at the reception so I can get my white dream machine."

"You and your white bike," he laughs.

"Hey, a girl's got to dream."

Backfire just drags me into his arms for a hug and holds me close.

"Do you really think your parents would object to an amazing man like me?"

I grin and shake my head no.

"And mine already love you. They see you as some sort of miracle worker," he smiles at me, "They'd pretty much given up on me settling down."

"How would they feel about limiting the numbers of distant relatives you haven't seen since you were three, or have never even met, to the wedding?" I ask.

"Let them try," he rumbles.

"Best we come up with a budget for the wedding and work with that, then we can see how many people we can have. Could you talk to Ace about how many non-members he is comfortable having around the clubhouse?"

"Yeah, babe. This isn't going to be easy, is it?"

"Nothing in life worth having is ever really easy," I tell him. "Let's just say if we plan this well, it should be relatively easy."

"I suppose we'd better go to the County Clerk to get a license then and set up the other hoops we have to go through. We have to do a fuckin' course about divorce before we can get married I think, according to the online research I did. That's the way it is."

"Like everything else in life, just loving each other isn't enough for us to get married. Someone always puts out more obstacles."

CHAPTER 30
STARTING TO TAKE
SHAPE

Kat

It's a pretty good thing that the bike did well at the local show. In fact, we all had a brilliant time and everyone got lots of new business contacts. The plus side for me is that it's distracting Backfire from thinking about the wedding.

He just wants it done. What a romantic.

It's not even a really complicated wedding with lots of people taking part, but regardless, it takes some planning, and some seriously silly money for one day.

We have the groundwork set up. It's a mixture of biker and traditional, and I love it.

We're off to the airport to pick up my sister Jack. She has come over early to help with the last minute stuff and pre-wedding parties. I've also conned her into being a bridesmaid. It took some doing, like I may have threatened her with the whole matching satin dress thing just for being difficult. Amber would be the only one who would possibly go for that look, but I told the girls to go burgundy. The style was irrelevant, as long as they felt comfortable in their own outfit. Even leather jeans would do.

Wizz has made me an incredible fitted corset top of white and burgundy leather that is way more comfortable than an actual corset. I think I look amazing in it.

Just about everything is worked out, and now it's time to start the parties. Tomorrow night, all the ladies are going out to see some male strippers. Hen night, or bachelorette party, whatever you want to call it; no men are allowed. This brought about some raised eyebrows in the clubhouse when some of the men found out.

Jack comes through immigration and Backfire pays attention. My sister is beautiful and I'm used to men paying attention to her, even mine. It's not that she's trying to attract attention, it just happens.

We grab her bag off the luggage carousel and head out to my new car. Backfire bought it for me and it is built more like a tank than a sports car. It keeps him happy knowing that I'm safe. I struggle to get around him wanting me to drive a tank when I want to ride a bike, but just don't bother him with it. What he doesn't know doesn't hurt him.

I have to be a bit careful about money now. Backfire wants to buy everything I need. I have to maintain a little independence without offending him, and since he doesn't want to offend me either, it sort of works.

I allow him to drive my car this time, which he always wants to do anyway so I can talk to Jack. It's really good to see her. She's like me in looks I suppose, but she's a couple of inches taller and a lot more sophisticated. Her clothes are always more planned and elegant and she always wears makeup.

So with that being said, she's awesome. She rides a bike too, but her taste runs more toward superbikes. Jack is a bit of a speed freak who loves nothing more than taking her bike to a track day at Donington to see how fast she can go. She's even been to some tracks over in Europe. At the sort of rallies I like to go to, she'll sometimes come with me if she can do "run-what-you-brung" drag racing. Jack shares my love of books and is a University Librarian in Brum.

We are totally excited to see each other, not even pretending to care about Backfire understanding us. With our Brummie accents out in full force, he just looks at me like he doesn't know what he's gotten himself into. It's a hard life, I get it.

Backfire

Fuck me!

Kat's little sister is going to go down well at the clubhouse but sadly, I can pretty much take any bet that Trash will be all over her like a rash. Poor girl.

I love seeing Kat this excited and happy. It makes all these plans seem worth it. I grant you, we've often said "fuck it all, let's go to Vegas," a lot, but now we're getting close to the actual wedding date and I'm glad we didn't.

We get back home and yes, it's now my home too, and Kat starts dragging Jack around, showing her what she's done with the place. I carry Jack's bag into the newly defined guest room and leave them to it for a while. Anyway, I'm only catchin' every two out of three words...

I hear a couple of bikes and grin as Trash and Shades pull up. The girls come piling out to see them and it doesn't take long for Jack and Trash to hit it off. I just fuckin' knew it.

The five of us sit out in the yard in our new entertainment area. I get my grill on and the new beer fridge starts to do its job. Like Kat, Jack is a cider drinker, and so it's easy to see them mellow out. They're both tired anyway. Kat's been wound up about Jack coming and Jack has travelled all this way so it doesn't take much. We eat, drink and enjoy the evening. Doesn't get much better than this.

CHAPTER 31
HEN NIGHTS AND BACHELOR PARTIES

Kat

All the girls are meeting up at a local bar before the final assault on the strip club, but that sister of mine is rabble rousing.

"If we go to see a load of male strippers, all we'll get is overly tanned, overly muscled, shaven chested, oiled-up pretty boys," she states.

I can't argue the point. "So what's your alternative?" I ask her. "And just once, couldn't you have mentioned it sooner?"

"Well I only just thought about it." she says, "We could go and watch some female strippers and maybe even get some ideas. I've always fancied learning to pole dance."

Now why am I not surprised at that?

"I actually think that's a cool idea. Anyone else up for it?" I'm met with a load of grins and nods. Fair enough. "Where shall we go?"

"How about here?" Christine suggests, picking up a magazine with an advertisement regarding a reduced entry into a new strip club a couple of miles up the road. We all pile into our cars with our designated drivers.

Strippers, here we come.

Backfire

The club just opened a new strip joint so we're going there. We've just settled around our table when another large group arrives.

"Fuck me," Trash says laughing, "it's the girls."

Kat and the others stop dead in their tracks as all the brothers are laughing their asses off. The girls notice us too and start to make their way over.

"Hey Handsome," Jack says to Trash, "Great minds and all that."

"Hey, beautiful. What brings you here?"

"We didn't fancy the bloke strippers so we thought we'd watch the girls, see if we can pick up any tips."

"Well, pull up a chair, or better yet, sit on my knee."

That finished the guys off. Shades fell off his seat laughing, so Kat grabbed it while he was on the floor. She was laughing so much she nearly joined him. No fuckin way that's happening so I pull her over onto my knee.

"Hi," she says, cuddling into me. "This wasn't the plan. Why are you at this particular place?"

"The club owns it now, so we thought we'd check it out."

All the girls are moving to their men. Looks like separate bachelor/bachelorette night is a bust as I watch chairs and tables being moved together as the girls settle in.

A new dancer comes on stage and the ladies pay more attention to her than the guys do. We've all seen it before, but it doesn't look like they have. They whoop it up and when the stripper comes near, their money comes out, however they don't shove it down her remaining clothing, but club together. Jack takes it and goes over to hand her the lot. On her way back to us, Trash grabs her, pulling her to sit on his lap and holding her there. I've never fuckin' seen him like this. It's interesting.

The next stripper comes on and the girls once again watch in apparent fascination. I'm not fuckin' sure if it's a good thing or a bad thing, but at least we know what they're up to.

As the night progresses, one of the strippers approaches the table. Normally they'd be all over us, but they're staying away because our women are here. Fuckin' clever of them, I'll say.

"Hey all," she says, "my stripper name is Blitz, but my real name is Dawn. Is everyone alright? I heard you may have some questions for us?"

At this I feel Kat's interest in what she has to say, as she and Jack exchange glances.

"Hi, Dawn. My name is Kat, and this is my hen night, or bachelorette party. We've gone a bit off plan, but can I ask where you learnt to dance? A few of my girls are interested in learning."

I grip her hard at this and hear rumbles of disapproval from guys around the table.

"We're just looking to learn how to pole dance, nothing more." Kat says to ease the tension from the guys.

Why am I not surprised at that? What does surprise me is Ace.

"If you ladies are interested in learning to pole dance, you can use this club in the mornings," he says.

The ladies cheer, all excited at the concept. Their men look bemused; I know where they're coming from.

"That would be so awesome," says Kat, her eyes shining.

"I can teach you," says Dawn, "I'm a qualified instructor."

"Awesome," Jack says, full of excitement.

"Why are you so pleased? You're going back to England," Kat demands.

"Well I might stay for a bit," Jack responds. Fuck me if I don't see the smile Trash can't quite hide. Kat, however, doesn't see anything but the opportunity to spend more time with her sister and she really starts to get her party on.

I realize she's been holding back on her party so I ask Jack about it. She grins at me and says "She didn't want to get too drunk in case someone did something to her. You know, covered her in condoms, got her a male stripper. Those sorts of things."

"And who would she suspect of such a thing?" I ask her.

"I have no idea," she says with a nearly straight face. "But she's partying now."

Oh yeah, that she is.

CHAPTER 32
FAMILY GATHERING

Backfire

It's just over a week 'til the wedding and my parents ride in. My pops rides his bike while Mom drives the car, no doubt full of wedding shit.

As Pops is a member of such long standing, Ace has offered them room at the clubhouse, but they've decided to stay at the hotel where most of the wedding party are staying and the catering is coming from.

We've agreed to introduce my pops and me to Kat's parents with our real names.

Because everyone wanted to meet them, we arrive at Tampa Airport in two cars. There are my parents, Kat, Jack, and Trash, whatever the fuck that's all about, and me. We hang out in the Harley shop waiting for them to clear customs and immigration.

By the time they get through, Kat hasn't spent too much money so that's something.

I go to help grab their bags. We load up and head back over the Bay to the hotel. We start to do introductions over a bite to eat.

Kat's dad's name is Colin and her mother's name is Amy. While Kat and Jack talk to their parents and mine, Trash and I haul their cases to their room. We come back and everyone seems to be getting along, sitting and chilling. Kat's parents have more than a snack 'cause the plane food was weird. It doesn't look like Jack had mentioned much about Trash to her folks so they're looking rather confused at this relationship. I see this as less pressure on me.

Colin's an architect and Amy's a college lecturer in history. As the conversation progresses, we discover that he's picked up a love of bikes from his daughters and had acquired Kat's old BSA, which is a great icebreaker. Kat's mom, being a history lecturer, fits in with my folks interest in medieval England. We arrange to take Colin out for a ride with us tomorrow while the ladies have agreed to hit the mall, mentioning scary shit like eyebrow threading and make-up. Better them than me.

CHAPTER 33

HAPPY, HAPPY, HAPPY -
YIKES

Kat

Oh my God, I couldn't be happier! The idea of getting married to Backfire is pretty unbelievable. I love him, and it's as simple as that.

But will it work?

Can we live and love together? Work and play together practically twenty-four hours a day, seven days a week?

Is it too much?

Without the odd kidnapping and shooting to make him go all Mr. Protector on me, will he get bored?

Do we need to put some distance between us? How? Everything I do is linked to him in some way. What if we burn up and burn out?

How the hell do I keep things exciting and interesting for him? I suppose the only thing I can do is work things out as they come along. I can make this work. I *will* make this work.

Worrying won't help me. It is what it is, so it's best to go with the flow and keep trying. At the very least, we'll have a hell of a ride together.

Backfire

I get home from work to see Kat nearly freaked out about something. I worry that the Dead have got to her in some way until she runs into my arms, crying about how she's sure we'll burn out 'cause we're 'too close all the time,' or some such shit.

I say to her, "Eyes on me, babe. Are you mine?"

"Yes," she squeaks with her eyes still brimming with tears.

"Am I yours?"

"Of course," she replies, "but…"

"No buts, babe," I tell her, "We face shit together and ride it out."

She relaxes a little at that, so I scoop her up and carry her to the bedroom. Words aren't enough for me to make my point, so when I toss her to the bed, I rip her tee off before she lands on the bed. She sits up to look at me and I grab the waist of her jeans to pull them off too. As I drop my jeans and release my cock, I see a hint of her smile again. I step to the edge of the bed and she wraps her legs round my waist, rubbing against my cock while I strip off my cut and my shirt. That gets her wetter and me harder so I lift her up and drive inside her in one motion. Fuck, it's good to be inside my woman.

I hold her arms over her head and lock our gazes as I fuck her hard. She writhes under me and shrieks my name as she comes, clamping around my cock.

"I'm yours, Backfire" she says with no doubt in her voice.

That's what I needed to hear. A few more deep thrusts and we come together.

CHAPTER 34
THE LAST GASP OF FREEDOM

Kat

Tomorrow is the day.

I miss being with Backfire. I tell myself it's only for one night, but that's not really helping. Silly superstitions. At least Jack and Trash are here, helping me deal with the final arrangements for the wedding and my nerves.

Bridezilla? Me?

Trash has the wedding phone so he can 'sort out' annoying queries. This fact has deterred everyone from trying it on.

Ace has made Jack welcome at the club and we have finalised the public areas and made sure the numbers are right.

The blood families are mixing and starting to get to know each other – our moms have been shopping and our dads have been riding. Loads of club family are starting to arrive too and everyone seems to be getting along, which is great because anyone who causes a drunken fight at my wedding will incur the wrath of Bullet, and any other Sergeants at Arms that arrive.

I am a bit gutted for Backfire that his two blood brothers haven't managed to make it so far due to club business. He seemed a bit down about that for a while, but then let it go. I have left some seats empty just in case. We both have family and friends that we've been unable to contact, who, if they turned up, would be more than welcome.

The only big mistake in the planning I nearly made was by not understanding the importance of a rehearsal dinner, but luckily I was told in time and the hotel was able to come through for us. The three families all mixed and had a great time. There was no one putting a spanner in the works and that's fine with me.

We are having the actual wedding at the clubhouse, so that's where Backfire is. I love the fact that you can get married just about anywhere here. We've planned for a mixture of different things. There are loads of different foods for after, hence why the formal wedding rehearsal had escaped me.

Everyone who can be here is here. Everything is ready for us to move on with tomorrow.

CHAPTER 35

THE DAY

Backfire

I wake up in my room at the clubhouse on my own 'cause of some shit about 'no seeing each other before the ceremony.' What that fuckin' translates to is not sleeping with Kat last night and I fuckin' hate it.

I shower and get dressed for the day. Luckily, my woman has an understanding of the whole biker thing and so my jeans might be new, but they are jeans. Same as my black, button-down shirt and boots; both new, but wearable. I head out to the kitchen to look for something to eat.

The ladies have put out a spread for breakfast. I get a plate and start to eat. Sadly, Sock and Shades turn up to start running their mouths, trying to ruin my day. What the fuck was I thinking, makin' Shades my best man? I did this to myself.

"And so the condemned man eats a hearty last meal," Sock starts in.

Before Shades even gets a chance, I slug him in the gut. Simple, 'cause he'll never learn.

Ace wanders in to add his two cents, "Whatever happens, don't hit each other in the face or you'll all have Kat to deal with, and she has Bullet on her side."

We all look at Bullet who just smiles slowly at us. Scary shit.

Kat

Jack and I are up and out early in the morning. We get breakfast and then we're off to get the final touches to our hair done.

We take off to the hotel and start getting everyone prepared for make-up and getting their clothing together. Once we have everyone taken care of and the parents away in cars, escorted by Liam on his bike, we go to our bikes.

The wedding bikes for Jack and I are beautiful. Mine is white and Jack's is burgundy and white. Everyone is starting to head out when we hear the rumble of what sounds like a thousand Harleys. Jack and I check out the parade of Cycle Devils, led by Ace and Snack. Brewer is giving Amber a ride and Lori rides her bike beside her man. Within moments, we're surrounded by Cycle Devils from different chapters—even Nomads.

Ace and Snack come forward, as do Seamus and Ultan. YES! I look to Ace for an explanation and he says, "You didn't think we'd let you arrive at your own wedding without an escort, did you?"

"Please, Ace. I don't want to cry, especially not yet and hopefully not at all." The bikers within hearing range quietly giggle.

Seamus and Ultan smile at me and reach out to hug me. They both make sure to kiss Jack.

Ultan grins at me and says, "Not even we would kiss you today, not without our brother's express permission."

"You came to meet me instead of going to be with Backfire?"

"Our brother will appreciate that we've come to escort you to him," Seamus says. "So, are you ready to take your ride to him?"

My smile is so big my face hurts, "Oh yes." I say.

Tex gives his instructions. "So it's like this, Kat. Snack and Ace will lead. You will ride beside Templar while Jack will ride beside Vike. Then Brewer will be with Lori and Amber. The rest of the brothers will follow in a coordinated ride behind us.

I grab both Ace and Snack and give them my attempt at a bear hug. Once I release them from my grip, I shout out to all the others, "Hello and Welcome. I hope you all enjoy the party."

They all roar in approval. The procession lines up in the allocated order, and we slowly start to ride toward the clubhouse.

Backfire

My bike is parked at the side of the wedding area with Shades', Trash's and Pop's. It has a traditional aisle covered in white flowers between two seating areas and a white arch at the back that looks traditional, until you look close and see it's decorated with loads of little white bikes. I know the girls have been making them for weeks. There's a small band to play wedding music, but who can also play country and rock music afterwards.

The seating area is full of our blood families, but none of the club is present. Just as that thought crosses my mind, I start to hear the loud rumble of bikes.

It gets louder and louder until the bikes appear, and in the lead is Kat and Ace. She looks so fuckin' fine my heart stops for a second.

The group splits into two. A small group parks their bikes by mine while the rest fill up the space in the background and start to fill up the chairs that are left. When the seats are full, apart from those at the front, they stand around the sides. Colin walks to the back of the aisle between the seats, and that's where Ace delivers a smiling Kat to her father.

The Bridal party starts to form up. Most of the guys go to their seats, apart from Ultan and Seamus, who come up to give me a bro hug. I'm so fuckin' happy they made it as I watch them go over to sit by our parents.

The wedding march begins to play and Kat walks up the aisle on Colin's arm toward me. The wedding service is very traditional until we get to the final vow, which is all about leather and Harleys. It appears that someone's been watching too many episodes of Sons of Anarchy.

Still, the laughter is a stress relief and everyone relaxes. I am now officially a married man. Fuck it, I'm happy.

Kat

When we promise to look after each other as much as our leather and ride each other as often as our bikes, the place erupts into laughter. That was the point; to make people relax.

The photographers start but we have left loads of little cameras about the place, along with things like bubble jars in place of confetti. I don't want Ace after me to tidy up the clubhouse grounds because that's not happening.

As people start to gather around, the Florida prospects start to take down the temporary fencing and a traditional funfair is revealed, along with a food fair of different types of cuisine spread out around it in various food trucks. There are strawberries and cream, and even Pimm's.

Everyone begins to dig in and help themselves. We plan the cake cutting for later in the area the wedding took place. As soon as the photos are taken, the next stage for the area is set up. Underneath the chairs, an area's been planked for dancing and music.

Throughout the grounds, various seating areas have been set up so people can sit and relax. At the back of the clubhouse, there is an area set up for bike games. The main two games are 'potato in the haystack', with better prizes than spuds and 'slow race'. I challenged Backfire to a slow race. He hasn't got the patience so I won easily, and we also won a prize in the haystack. Backfire's prize was to remove the hay from my cleavage.

Everything is set up to perfection for a wedding such as this. I couldn't have asked for anything better than this day.

Backfire

I laugh as Kat and her girls go on the carousel again, realizing that this is Kat's new toy. Trash and Jack have been on 'bite the wienie' and 'in the haystack' several times.

I have my brothers on either side of me, catching up and having fun. I think that the best way to describe this day is by saying that it's fuckin' awesome.

CHAPTER 36
PILLOW TALK

Kat

"I love you," I tell him as we curl up to sleep on our wedding night.

"Not as much as I love you," he says as he reaches behind him to pull two glasses of Jack off the bedside cabinet.

"To our future," he toasts.

"To our future," I agree.

EPILOGUE

Backfire

It's club night and Ace starts to tell us about a new club plan, "The Cycle Devils are going to patch over an English club," he says. "Because our chapter has links to England, we have been asked to send members over to meet the UK club. Meeting Kat and Jack has taught us that there are a load of differences between our cultures, so we wondered if Backfire and Trash would like to go over there as part of our party with their old ladies as unofficial translators, all expenses on the club."

Trash grins at Ace, "That sounds amazing. I'll go, and Jack has shit to sort over there anyhow."

"Backfire?" Ace asks.

"We're getting a bike ready to show at Daytona. I'll obviously go where the club wants, but I don't know if Kat can come. She has to get it painted."

"Shit," Ace says, "We need to find out how to make the timelines work. I'll find out a timetable, you sort one out too, Backfire. We need to make this work to get Kat out of the picture in case the Dead or the consortium make a move on her."

"It'll be an epic honeymoon if we can manage it."

England here we come.

A story to be told in the next Cycle Devils book,

What the Devil Wants

ACKNOWLEDGEMENTS

Really there are too many people to thank here, so I'm going to stick to the main ones.

My husband Martin

For being wonderful and so much help.

Ava Manello

For making me believe that an ordinary person like me could write a book.

Dana Hook

Editor Extraordinaire.

Margreet Asselbergs

Artist beyond compare.

Lori

For being my mate.

Ryder Dane

For re-focussing me when I was losing the plot.

Sam and Lena

My beta readers for their time and suggestions.

ABOUT THE AUTHOR

Hi – my name is Clare, and although it shocks me, I'm an author...

I'm English and consider myself a biker, whether you do or not is up to you. I come from the Midlands, but have moved up North (!)

I started to ride bikes in 1980, and have been around bikes and bikers ever since.

I've loads of interests and hobbies but particularly I ride and drive horses and craft.

You can contact me via :

Clare Power Books

http://clarepower.blogspot.co.uk/

Clare Power's Book Riding Babes

https://www.facebook.com/groups/729477027129814/